Under the Okanagan Sun i

Under the Okanagan Sun i

Constance Santego

Under the Okanagan Sun

Dr. Constance Santego weaves stories of love, history, and personal transformation set against the breathtaking landscapes of British Columbia. Living most of her life in the heart of Canada's Okanagan Valley, she draws inspiration from the beauty around her to create compelling narratives that explore the intricacies of the human spirit. Constance shares a fulfilling life with her husband, and her work reflects her passion for storytelling, healing, and the enduring power of connection.

www.constancesantego.ca

iv   Constance Santego

Published by
Editor & Interior Layout: Dr. Constance Santego
Book Layout: ©2017 BookDesignTemplates.com
Soft Cover ISBN: 978-1-990062-59-9

eBook ISBN: 978-1-990062-60-5

Created and published in Canada. Printed and bound in the United States of America
Ordering Information: csantego@gmail.com

ALSO BY DR. CONSTANCE SANTEGO

NOVELS
Illegitimate Grace

Okanagan Trilogy:
Beneath the Vineyards

The Nine Spiritual Gifts Series:
Journey of a Soul – (Vol 1 Michael)
Language of a Soul – (Vol 2 Gabriel)
Prophecy of a Soul – (Vol 3 Bath Kol)
Healing of a Soul – (Vol 4 Raphael)
Miracles of a Soul – (Vol 5 Hamied)
Knowledge of a Soul – (Vol 6 Raziel)
Wisdom of a Soul – (Vol 7 Uriel)
Faith of a Soul – (Vol 8 Pistis Sophia)

NONFICTION
The Intuitive Life, The Gift Of Prophecy, Third
Edition
Fairy Tales, Dreams And Reality… Where Are You On
Your Path? Second Edition
Your Persona… The Mask You Wear
Archangel Michael's Soul Retrieval Guide
Tesla And The Future Of Energy Medicine
Beyond Tesla: *Advancing The Science Of Energy Healing*
Tesla's Code: *Mastering Energy, Frequency, And Creative
Power*
Scaling Beyond 6 Figures: *Strategies for Health & Wellness
Professionals*
Beyond the Mind: *Harnessing the Power of Astral Projection
for Creative Awakening*
Bend, Don't Break: *Finding Your Way Back to Abundance*
Ring Therapy: *A Guide to Healing and Balance*
Ring Therapy Pocket Guide

Floraopathy™: *The Art and Science of Vibrational Healing with Essential Oils*

REIKI WISDOM, SERIES:
The Reiki Master's Manual
Angelic Lifestyle, a Vibrant Lifestyle
Angelic Lifestyle 42-Day Energy Cleanse
Reiki and the Power of The Joint Points: *Unlocking Energy Pathways for Healing*

SECRETS OF A HEALER, SERIES:
Magic Of Aromatherapy (Vol I)
Magic Of Reflexology (Vol II)
Magic Of The Gifts (Vol III)
Magic Of Muscle Testing (Vol IV)
Magic Of Iridology (Vol V)
Magic Of Massage (Vol VI)
Magic Of Hypnotherapy (Vol VII)
Magic Of Reiki (Vol VIII)
Magic Of Advanced Aromatherapy (Vol IX)
Magic Of Esthetics (Vol X)
The Reiki Master's Manual (Vol XI)

ADULT COLORING JOURNALS
SERIES-ZEN COLORING:
Quantum Energy and Mindful Living Journal (Vol 1)
Reiki Energy Journal (Vol 2)
Nine Spiritual Gifts Journal (Vol 3)
I Forgive Journal (Vol 4)

SERIES – COLORING PROSPERITY:
Genie-Inspired Mandalas and Wealth Journal (Vol 1)
Entrepreneurial Mindset Reboot (Vol 2)

SERIES – HARMONIC MIND CODE:
Harmonic Mind Code Coloring Journal (Vol 1)

FOR CHILDREN
I am Big Tonight. I Don't Need the Light

Dedicated

To the land of the Okanagan and its people—past, present, and future. Your beauty, resilience, and stories inspire this journey. This book is a tribute to the enduring connection between the heart, the land, and the legacy we leave behind.

Under the Okanagan Sun

Emily Carter: A Story of Healing and Heritage

In the heart of the Okanagan Valley, Emily Carter arrives searching for renewal. A talented landscape photographer facing the fallout of a failed business venture, she returns to Kelowna, British Columbia, Canada—a place of sparkling lakes, rolling vineyards, and the whisper of second chances.

Emily's journey unfolds as she is drawn into the vibrant rhythms of the valley, capturing its beauty through her lens. Amid this scenic wonder, she encounters Liam Fraser, a gifted artisan boatbuilder restoring the region's maritime heritage. His passion for craftsmanship and the land's history stirs something long dormant in Emily's heart.

As Emily discovers hidden letters revealing an untold love story from the past, she begins to see the parallels between preserving the valley's heritage and reclaiming her own dreams. Her bond with Liam grows as they navigate the tensions between progress and tradition, finding in each other the strength to embrace life's uncertainties.

This is a story of restoration—of land, love, and self—set against the breathtaking backdrop of Kelowna's lakes and vineyards. A tribute to the courage it takes to heal and the timeless connections that shape us, Emily's journey is a reminder that beauty and love often emerge from life's most unexpected moments.

The roots of our past anchor us,

but it is in tending to them—honoring
their stories and nurturing their
legacy—that we find the strength to
heal, grow, and chart our own course
into the future."

Dr. Constance Santego

xvi   Constance Santego

Fact and Disclaimer:

This novel draws upon the rich beauty and cultural heritage of the Okanagan Valley to create a fictional narrative of love, healing, and personal discovery. While real locations and elements of the region's traditions are featured, all characters, events, and specific scenarios are entirely the product of the author's imagination.

The story aims to offer readers a heartfelt exploration of the human spirit, set against the stunning backdrop of Kelowna's vineyards, lakes, and vibrant community. It reflects themes of resilience, connection, and the courage to embrace life's unexpected turns.

Any resemblance to actual persons, living or deceased, or real events is purely coincidental.

Prologue

The sun dipped low over the tranquil waters of Okanagan Lake, painting the sky in hues of gold and rose. The gentle rustle of the breeze through the pines harmonized with the lapping waves, creating a melody only this valley could compose. Here, where the land and lake converged, life moved at its own pace, unhurried and timeless, as though the earth itself held its breath to honor the stories buried in its soil.

I came to this place not in search of answers but to escape the weight of questions I could no longer bear. My photography, once a source of pride and purpose, had become a hollow routine. Calgary, with its unrelenting bustle and expectations, had drained me of my passion, leaving only the shadow of the artist I once was.

In this valley of storied vineyards and glimmering waters, I sought solitude, a quiet refuge where I could remember who I was— or perhaps discover who I might yet become. What I didn't anticipate was the pull of the land itself or the people it would bring into my life.

And then there was him.

Liam Fraser, a man as deliberate and steady as the craft he practiced. His hands, calloused from years of shaping wood into vessels that danced upon the lake, seemed to carry not just skill, but the history of a place and its people. He was not a man of many words, but his presence spoke volumes. Through his quiet determination and unwavering connection to the valley, he began to reveal to me something I'd long forgotten—the courage to hope.

This is not a tale of grand gestures or epic transformations. It is a story of small, meaningful moments—of hands smoothing weathered wood, of letters uncovered in the quiet corners of a cabin, and of moonlit walks that speak of possibilities. It is about the courage to trust the stillness, to let the land heal you, and to believe that even broken dreams can be reimagined.

Before you judge the choices that brought us here, understand this: the strength to begin again often lies not in the answers we seek, but in the unexpected paths that find us.

Sometimes, it is in the soft light of the Okanagan sun and the quiet persistence of a heart that we rediscover the stories we were always meant to live.

Chapter 1

The rhythmic hum of tires on the highway was the only sound accompanying Emily Carter as she navigated the winding roads that skirted the edge of Mara Lake. The golden light of late afternoon danced across the water's surface, its gentle ripples catching the sun like shards of broken glass. She had forgotten how British Columbia seemed to hold its own kind of magic, a place where time slowed, and the weight of the world felt a little lighter.

She wasn't moving to the Okanagan by choice—at least, not entirely. Leaving Calgary, with its relentless pace and gleaming skyline, had been a reluctant necessity. Losing her photography studio, the venture she had poured every ounce of herself into, was a blow she hadn't fully processed. The city that had once felt full of promise had turned into a place of relentless pressure, until there was nothing left to give.

The small cabin she had found online seemed like the perfect escape. Nestled near Okanagan Lake, surrounded by towering pines and sagebrush-covered hills, it promised the isolation Emily craved more than she was willing to admit.

Driving there, however, was an entirely different experience. Westside road between Vernon and Kelowna was both a test of patience and nerve. The narrow, winding road clung to the rugged cliffs that hugged the lake, each hairpin turn offering breathtaking views—and a stark reminder to keep both hands firmly on the wheel.

Emily had taken it slow, her little car hugging the curves as the road dipped and climbed with the terrain. To her leftt, the shimmering expanse of Okanagan Lake stretched endlessly, its waters catching the sun in a dance of light. To her right, steep hillsides rose dramatically, dotted with sagebrush, weathered pines, and stubborn clusters of wildflowers clinging tenaciously to the rocky soil.

Each turn revealed something new—a secluded cove, a hidden beach, or the fleeting movement of wildlife darting across the hillside. The drive wasn't easy, but Emily welcomed the challenge. There was something grounding in the road's imperfections, its refusal to smooth out for convenience. It reminded her of life—unpredictable, messy, and, at times, breathtakingly beautiful.

As she left the highway and followed the signs toward Fintry, the world seemed to grow quieter. The road narrowed even further, flanked by dense forests that let in only slivers of sunlight. She had read about Fintry in her research—a historic area once home to a sprawling estate and now a provincial park. The promise of quiet seclusion had drawn her here, to a cabin that overlooked both the lake and the park's natural beauty.

As she pulled into the gravel driveway, the cabin came into view. It was modest, with weathered cedar siding and a small porch where a pair of rocking chairs waited beneath the shade of a sloping roof. Ivy crept up one side of the structure, and a collection of firewood was stacked neatly against the other. It wasn't much, but it was enough.

Emily stepped out of her car, stretching after the long drive, and inhaled deeply. The air smelled of pine and earth, tinged with a faint sweetness she couldn't place. For a moment, she let herself savor it, the quiet and the open space a stark contrast to the chaos she had left behind.

Inside, the cabin was just as simple. The living room held a threadbare sofa—a sofa so old and worn to the point where the fabric has become thin, faded, and frayed, a wood fireplace, and a woodstove, while the small kitchen was equipped with mismatched dishes and an ancient gas stove. A single bedroom, barely large enough to hold a bed and dresser, completed the space. Yet, there was something charming about its unpolished edges, a kind of unspoken invitation to make it her own.

Unpacking felt like an act of defiance. Each box she opened, each item she placed on a shelf, was a quiet declaration that she could start over, even if she wasn't sure how. Her camera equipment, carefully packed in its padded cases, was the last thing she unpacked. She hesitated before placing it on the small desk by the window.

The camera had been her lifeline for as long as she could remember. It had taken her to places she had never imagined and told stories for which she didn't have the words. But now, it felt like a stranger—a reminder of everything she had lost.

As the sun dipped lower, Emily stepped onto the porch, a cup of tea warming her hands. The lake stretched out before her, calm and steady, its surface catching the last rays of daylight. Somewhere in the distance, the faint sound of a loon's call echoed across the water.

This was why she had come—to find stillness, to listen for something she couldn't yet name. The valley, with its rugged beauty and quiet resilience, felt like a place where she might piece herself back together.

For now, that would have to be enough.

Chapter 2

The rhythmic sound of a scraper plane gliding over wood filled the air inside Liam Fraser's boathouse. Dust motes danced in the shafts of sunlight streaming through the wide barn doors, their glow softening the rough edges of the workbench strewn with tools. Liam paused, wiping the sweat from his brow with the back of his hand, and stepped back to inspect his work.

The sailboat was a beauty, even in her current state of disrepair. Her lines were graceful, her hull strong and proud, though scarred by years of neglect. She was the kind of boat that held stories in her planks—of adventures, of family outings on the lake, and perhaps even of heartbreak. To Liam, restoring her wasn't just a project, it was a way of giving those stories a second life.

His hands, calloused from years of craftsmanship, moved over the wood like they belonged there. Each stroke of the plane, each turn of the clamp, brought her closer to the vision he held in his mind. This wasn't just any sailboat, it was a Lady of the Lake, one of the few wooden vessels remaining from the early days of Okanagan Lake's maritime history.

The Lady's history fascinated Liam. She had been built in the 1920s by a local shipwright who had crafted boats for the orchardists and families who depended on the lake for transportation and trade. She had seen summers filled with laughter and winters spent moored, enduring the valley's icy winds. Restoring her wasn't just about the craft—it was about preserving a piece of the Okanagan's soul.

Outside, the view of the lake framed the boathouse's open doors like a living painting. The water sparkled beneath the mid-morning sun, and the distant hills stood in muted greens and browns. The boathouse itself was a relic, built by Liam's grandfather when boats were still a lifeline for the valley's remote communities. The scent of cedar and varnish mingled with the faint tang of the lake air, grounding Liam in the work he loved.

He had moved back to the Okanagan after years of city life, drawn by a need to reconnect with something real. The corporate architecture world had left him burnt out, and the endless deadlines and profit-driven projects felt increasingly hollow. Here, working with his hands and preserving the past, he had found a sense of purpose he hadn't realized he was missing.

As he worked, his mind wandered to the idea of expanding his craft. He had been toying with the idea of offering boat-building workshops—inviting people to experience the satisfaction of shaping wood into something that could ride the waves. But it was a daunting thought. Teaching others meant stepping out of the solitary rhythm he had come to rely on.

"Looks like you're getting there, old girl," he muttered, running a hand over the boat's smoothed keel.

The sound of footsteps crunching on gravel pulled Liam from his thoughts. A moment later, a familiar figure appeared in the doorway—Ethan Montgomery, his oldest friend and the proud owner of one of the valley's most celebrated wineries, a reputation solidified after Claire Bennett's article was published.

Ethan carried two cups of coffee, a grin spreading across his sun-worn face. "Thought you could use a break," he said, handing one to Liam.

Liam accepted it with a nod of thanks, leaning back against the workbench as Ethan surveyed the progress on the *Lady of the Lake*.

"She's coming along," Ethan remarked, his tone tinged with admiration. "I can already picture her out on the water again."

"Me too," Liam replied, taking a sip of coffee. "It's slow work, but worth it."

Ethan chuckled. "That's you in a nutshell—patient and persistent. You know, not everyone sees the value in bringing the past back to life."

Liam shrugged. "It's not just about the boat. It's about what she represents. This lake has a history, Ethan. It's worth remembering."

Ethan nodded, his expression turning thoughtful. "Speaking of history, I've got a photographer coming to document the harvest this year. New to the area, from Calgary. Maybe she'd be interested in what you're doing here."

Liam raised an eyebrow. "A photographer?"

"Yeah, Emily Carter. She's renting a place near here. Seems like she could use a fresh start, kind of like you."

Liam didn't say anything, but he couldn't help but wonder about Emily Carter. He wasn't the type to seek out new connections, preferring the simplicity of his own company and the rhythm of his work. But something about Ethan's tone made him curious.

"Well," Ethan said, finishing his coffee. "I should let you get back to it. Just thought you should know—you're not the only one chasing something new in this valley."

Liam watched as Ethan set his empty coffee cup on the workbench, a glint of curiosity in his friend's eyes as he studied the boat.

"So," Ethan said, running a hand along the smoothed planks of the hull, "How much longer until she's ready to hit the water?"

"A while," Liam replied, wiping his hands on a rag. "But I could finish a lot sooner if I had some help."

Ethan chuckled, holding up his hands. "Oh no, I know where this is going. You're about to recruit me, aren't you?"

Liam smirked, already reaching for a spare Jack plane on the bench. "You're the one who showed up uninvited, so you might as well make yourself useful. I've got this section that needs smoothing out. Think you can handle it?"

Ethan hesitated, then took the hand tool with a dramatic sigh. "Fine. But don't blame me if I ruin your precious Lady of the Lake."

"You won't," Liam said confidently, guiding Ethan to the section he'd been working on. "Just follow the grain. Small strokes."

Ethan laughed as he gave it a tentative try. The motion was awkward at first but gradually steady under Liam's quiet instructions. The two worked side by side for a while, the silence broken only by the rhythmic sound of tools on wood and the occasional comment from Ethan about how hard the work was.

"See?" Liam said after a while, stepping back to inspect Ethan's progress. "Not bad. Maybe I'll make a craftsman out of you yet."

Ethan grinned, handing back the tool. "Don't count on it. I'll stick to grapes, thank you very much. But I'll admit—there's something satisfying about it. I can see why you do this."

Liam nodded, watching as Ethan brushed the sawdust from his hands and headed back to his truck. As the crunch of gravel faded into the background, Liam turned back to the boat. The sight of the freshly smoothed planks made him smile.

Chapter 3

Emily wandered along the narrow trail that meandered close to the edge of Okanagan Lake. The crisp air carried the scent of pine and the faint tang of the water. She had ventured out from her cabin that morning, camera in hand, hoping to capture the interplay of light and shadow as the sun climbed higher in the sky.

The trail opened up near a clearing, and ahead, tucked into the curve of the shore, was a structure she hadn't expected to see—a boathouse. Weathered cedar shingles glinted faintly in the sunlight, and wide barn-style doors stood open, revealing the skeleton of a boat resting in the middle of the workshop. The sound of a hammer striking wood echoed faintly, steady and rhythmic.

Curiosity pulled her closer. She wasn't sure what compelled her to step inside, but there was something magnetic about the scene—the quiet industriousness of the workshop, the contrast of order and creativity. She lingered just beyond the open doors, camera hanging loosely around her neck, taking it all in.

"Looking for something?" a deep voice startled her.

Emily stepped back instinctively, her cheeks flushing. The man who had spoken stood just inside the doorway, tools in hand. He was tall, with broad shoulders that seemed built for the kind of work this boathouse demanded. His dark brown hair was tousled, streaked with traces of sawdust, and a hint of stubble lined his sharp jaw. His sleeves were rolled up, exposing forearms marked by faint scars and calluses—evidence of years spent working with wood and tools.

His eyes, a piercing shade of green, held a mix of curiosity and caution, as though he wasn't quite sure what to make of her. Though his expression wasn't unkind, there was a quiet intensity about him, as though he carried the weight of his thoughts even in silence.

"I'm sorry," she said quickly. "I didn't mean to intrude. I was just out walking and—well, this place caught my eye."

Liam raised an eyebrow, glancing briefly at the camera around her neck. "You must be the photographer Ethan was talking about."

Emily offered a hesitant smile, brushing a strand of auburn hair behind her ear. Her hair, slightly windblown from the walk, framed a face that was striking in its simplicity—light freckles dusted her nose and cheeks, and her gray-blue eyes carried a depth that suggested she saw more than most. She wore a practical jacket and sturdy boots, her appearance unassuming but purposeful, as though she belonged in places like this—quiet, natural, and full of stories waiting to be uncovered.

Her brows furrowed. "Ethan?"

"The winery. He mentioned hiring someone to document the harvest. Guess that's you."

Emily relaxed slightly, grateful for the connection. "Yes, that's me. Emily Carter." She extended a hand, and after a moment, Liam set down his tools and shook it.

"Liam Fraser. This is my workshop," he said, gesturing toward the boathouse as if its contents explained everything.

She looked around, taking in the unfinished sailboat in the center of the room. "You're building that?"

"Restoring," he corrected, the faintest hint of pride in his voice. "It's a historic wooden sailboat. Been working on her for a while."

Emily's gaze swept over the boat, and her fingers itched to raise the camera. "She's beautiful. Do you mind if I—?"

He hesitated, his eyes flickering to the camera before landing on her face. "Go ahead. Just don't post anything without asking."

"Of course," Emily agreed, lifting the camera and framing a shot. She moved carefully, focusing on the interplay of the wood's grain and the way the light filtered through the open doors.

Liam watched her quietly, noting the way she moved with purpose, as if the act of capturing the image brought her some kind of clarity. She had an air of determination about her, the kind that made him wonder what stories she carried.

There was a natural ease to the way she moved, yet a flicker of something uncertain lingered in her expression, as though she wasn't just capturing the boat but searching for something deeper. Liam's gaze lingered a moment longer than he intended, struck by how seamlessly she seemed to fit into the scene.

When she lowered the camera, she met his gaze. "Thank you. I've never seen anything like this before. There's so much detail."

"It's slow work," Liam said, his tone neutral. "But it's worth it."

Emily nodded. "I'd love to learn more about the boat—its history, I mean. I'm sure it has a story to tell."

He studied her for a moment before giving a small nod. "Maybe next time. I've got to get back to it."

Taking the cue, Emily stepped back toward the trail, a slight smile tugging at her lips. "Thank you, Liam. I hope I'll see her finished one day."

"Maybe you will," he said, his tone unreadable.

As she walked back toward her cabin, Emily couldn't help but replay the encounter in her mind. Something about Liam Fraser intrigued her—not just his work, but the quiet intensity he carried.

Chapter 4

The cabin had begun to take on the scent of freshly brewed coffee, and the faint aroma of pine carried in on the breeze. Emily stood in the small kitchen, staring out the window as she cradled her mug. The view was postcard perfect—Okanagan Lake glinting in the morning light, flanked by hills dotted with evergreens. It was peaceful here, quiet in a way that felt almost foreign after years of city life.

Her unpacking had been slow, more a matter of necessity than excitement. Most of her things were still in boxes, shoved into the corner of the cabin's small living room. She told herself there was no rush—it wasn't like she had a tight deadline to meet or a boss breathing down her neck.

She set the mug down and walked to the desk by the window, where her camera rested.

The familiar weight of it in her hands brought a small sense of comfort, though it also carried a reminder of the pressure she'd felt in Calgary. There, photography had been a career, a business she'd poured her soul into, until it had all unraveled.

Emily sank into the worn chair, her fingers tracing the edges of the camera. She had loved her studio—loved the rush of working with clients, the challenge of capturing fleeting moments. But competition had been fierce, and no matter how hard she'd worked, it always seemed like someone else had more connections, more resources, more luck. The final blow came when her biggest client, a high-profile marketing firm, decided to go with another photographer. From there, the cancellations had snowballed until the studio was no longer viable.

The sting of failure still lingered, a dull ache that crept in during quiet moments like this. Coming back to Kelowna felt like admitting defeat, though she tried to frame it as a fresh start. Her parents had retired here years ago, and though they had since downsized to a condo in Vernon, the Okanagan Valley had always felt like a place to regroup.

She sighed, setting the camera back on the desk.

Determined not to spiral into self-pity, Emily decided to explore her surroundings. She grabbed her jacket and stepped outside, the crisp air immediately filling her lungs. The gravel path from her cabin led down to the lake, and she followed it, letting her boots crunch softly against the ground.

The lake stretched out before her, calm and steady, its surface broken only by the occasional ripple. The mountains on the far side rose with quiet strength, their ridges etched against the sky, softened by a morning haze that lingered over the lake. Emily snapped a few photos, the click of the shutter echoing in the stillness.

As she wandered further, she began to notice small details she'd missed before—a wildflower blooming stubbornly near the waterline, the way the light caught on the rippling waves, the faint outline of a fishing boat in the distance.

For the first time in what felt like forever, she allowed herself to slow down. There was no one waiting for her photos, and there was no looming deadline. She could take her time and let her lens rediscover the joy of simply capturing beauty for the sake of it.

By the time she returned to the cabin, her cheeks were flushed from the crisp air, and her spirits felt lighter. She set her camera back on the desk and sank onto the couch, feeling an unfamiliar mix of hope and trepidation.

Kelowna wasn't Calgary. There were few towering skyscrapers, no bustling clients clamoring for her attention. But maybe that was the point. Maybe this place, with its quiet rhythm and unassuming beauty, could teach her to listen again—not just to the world around her, but to herself.

The thought lingered as she gazed out the window at the lake. Perhaps there was still a story to tell here. Perhaps she wasn't as lost as she thought.

Chapter 5

Emily pulled her car onto a gravel driveway bordered by rows of grapevines stretching toward the horizon. A wooden sign near the entrance read: Evergreen Estates Winery. Family-Owned Since 1946. The sign's weathered paint and hand-carved lettering spoke of tradition, a legacy built with care and resilience.

She parked near a building with cedar shingles and large windows, its rustic charm blending seamlessly with the landscape. The air was warm with the scent of ripening grapes, sun-drenched earth, and the faint sweetness of fermenting wine. It was as though the land itself carried its own quiet rhythm, welcoming yet resolute.

Adjusting the strap of her camera bag, Emily stepped out of her car and took a deep breath. This meeting felt different—like more than just an interview. It was a chance to rediscover the passion she thought she'd lost. Ethan Montgomery, the owner, had sounded professional but measured on the phone, his tone hinting at someone who valued quality above all else.

The winery's front door creaked open before she could knock, and a man stepped out onto the porch. He looked to be in his mid-thirties, with dark, wavy hair and a sharp, observant gaze. His casual button-up shirt, rolled at the sleeves, and well-worn jeans hinted at someone accustomed to long hours outdoors.

"You must be Emily Carter," he said, his voice polite but guarded as he extended a hand. "Ethan Montgomery. Welcome to Evergreen Estates."

"Hi," Emily replied, shaking his hand. "Thanks for meeting with me. This place is stunning."

"Appreciate that," Ethan said with a slight nod. "We like to keep it true to what it's always been—a family vineyard. Let's take a walk, and I'll show you around."

They followed a gravel path winding through rows of grapevines, the fruit hanging heavy on the vines. Ethan's stride was purposeful, his words deliberate as he described the winery's history.

"My grandfather planted the first vines in the 1940s," he said, gesturing to a particularly dense section of the vineyard. "Most of what you see here is from his time—or replanted by my parents when they took over. Evergreen's small, but we've kept it that way for a reason. Quality over quantity."

Emily nodded, impressed by his dedication. "It's clear how much care goes into this place. You can feel it just walking through."

Ethan glanced at her, a flicker of approval crossing his face. "That's the idea. Evergreen isn't just about making wine—it's about preserving what this valley stands for. That's what I want you to capture. Not just the harvest, but the connection between the land, the people, and the process."

Emily adjusted the strap of her camera bag. "That's exactly the kind of story I want to tell. I want the images to feel authentic—like they belong here."

Ethan's steps slowed as they reached the edge of the vineyard, where the lake glimmered faintly in the distance. He turned to face her, his expression thoughtful but unreadable.

"I saw the samples you sent over," he said after a pause. "Good work. You've got the eye for this kind of thing. I'm willing to take a chance on you."

Emily blinked, caught off guard by his directness. "Thank you. I won't let you down."

"I'll hold you to that," Ethan replied, his tone firm but not unkind. "We're in the middle of harvest, so things are hectic. Be ready to start tomorrow. I'll introduce you to the crew in the morning, and we can go over the shots we need."

"Of course," Emily said quickly. "I'll be ready."

Ethan nodded once, and the conversation seemingly settled. "Feel free to walk around today and get a feel for the place. Just be careful around the equipment."

As he turned and headed back toward the main building, Emily stayed behind, her gaze sweeping over the vines and the hills beyond. She let her fingers drift to her camera, a spark of anticipation flaring to life.

This wasn't just a job—it was a chance to rebuild, to prove to herself that she could create something meaningful again. For the first time in a long time, hope flickered at the edges of her thoughts.

Chapter 6

After spending the morning wandering through the vineyard and snapping photos of its golden hues and sun-drenched vines, her thoughts kept drifting back to the boathouse she'd stumbled upon the day before. Something about Liam Fraser's quiet focus and the way he worked with the wood had left an impression she couldn't shake.

The afternoon light was perfect as she followed the trail that skirted the edge of the lake. The air was warm but carried the cool, earthy undertones of the water. The boathouse came into view, its weathered cedar siding blending seamlessly into the natural surroundings.

This time, Emily didn't linger outside. She stepped through the wide-open doors, camera slung over her shoulder. The rhythmic scrape of a scraper plane on wood greeted her, steady and deliberate, like a heartbeat for the space.

Liam was bent over the boat, his back to her, sleeves rolled up as he shaped one of the boat's ribs. His movements were fluid and practiced. She raised her camera, framing the shot carefully. The light caught on the sawdust, swirling in the air, creating a halo effect around him.

The shutter clicked, breaking the quiet.

Liam straightened and turned, his expression unreadable but his eyes sharp.

"You again," he said, setting the tool down on the workbench.

"I'm sorry," Emily said, stepping forward but stopping just inside the doorway. "I couldn't resist. This place—it's incredible."

Liam crossed his arms, his gaze flicking to her camera. "You could've asked."

"I know," she admitted, a faint flush creeping into her cheeks. "I got carried away. It won't happen again."

He studied her for a moment before sighing and gesturing toward the boat. "If you're going to be here, at least make yourself useful. Hand me that clamp."

Emily hesitated, then set her camera down on the workbench and picked up the clamp he'd pointed to. She handed it over, watching as he adjusted it carefully to hold the rib in place.

Emily tilted her head, studying the elegant lines of the boat. "Does she have a name?" she asked, her voice curious. She had heard that boats were often named after women, a tradition she found both charming and intriguing.

Liam glanced up, his lips curling into a faint smile. "She does," he said, running a hand along the hull. "Lady of the Lake. Built in the 1920s. She's one of the last wooden sailboats of her kind still around on Okanagan Lake."

Emily stepped closer, her eyes tracing the boat's graceful curves. "She's beautiful. What's her story?"

Liam leaned back slightly, resting his hands on his hips. "She used to carry passengers across the lake before there was a bridge. Boats like this were the lifeline for people in the valley. Now, she's just a memory—one I'm trying to keep alive."

"She's beautiful," Emily said, her gaze sweeping over the boat's smooth lines and the painstaking care evident in every detail.

"She will be," Liam corrected. "Once she's restored. Right now, she's still a mess."

Emily smiled faintly. "I think that's part of the beauty—seeing the process, how something broken can be rebuilt."

For the first time, Liam glanced at her, his expression softening slightly. "You sound like someone who knows a thing or two about rebuilding."

Emily's smile faltered for a split second before she recovered. "Maybe."

The silence stretched between them, but it wasn't uncomfortable. She picked up her camera again, glancing at him for permission. This time, he nodded.

"You can take a few photos," he said. "Just don't post anything online. I'm not looking for attention."

"Understood," Emily said, raising the camera.

As she moved around the boat, capturing the interplay of wood, light, and shadows, she couldn't help but feel a sense of connection— to the place, to the work being done here, and to the man behind it.

"So, what got you into this?" she asked, lowering the camera for a moment.

"Restoring boats?" Liam shrugged. "My grandfather built this boathouse back when the lake was a lifeline for the valley. Boats were everything back then—transportation, trade, connection. I grew up hearing his stories, and when I got tired of the city life in

Vancouver, this seemed like the right thing to come back to."

"Do you ever miss it? The city?"

"Not really," Liam said, picking up his hand tool again. "I've got everything I need here. The quiet, the craft. It's enough."

Emily nodded, understanding more than she expected.

"Thanks for letting me watch," she said after a while, slinging her camera strap over her shoulder. "I'll leave you to it."

"Stop by if you want more photos," Liam said, almost as an afterthought. "Just don't sneak up on me next time."

Emily laughed softly. "Deal."

As she stepped back into the sunlight, she felt a curious mix of calm and energy. There was something grounding about the boathouse, about Liam's steady presence.

Chapter 7

The morning air was crisp and alive with the scent of ripe grapes, earth, and the faint tang of crushed fruit. Emily stood near the edge of the vineyard at Evergreen Estates, her camera slung over her shoulder, observing the quiet buzz of activity around her. Workers moved between the rows of vines with precision, their laughter, and chatter weaving through the rustling leaves.

Ethan gave her a brief overview of the harvest process before sending her to explore and document. Now, watching the scene unfold, Emily was struck by how much care and attention went into every aspect of the work. This wasn't just about pulling grapes from the vines—it was about preserving a legacy.

She crouched low, framing a shot of a pair of hands delicately clipping a bunch of grapes from the vine. The deep purple fruit hung heavy, its skin glistening with dew in the morning light. The worker, a woman with sun-weathered skin and a warm smile, paused to look at Emily.

"Beautiful, aren't they?" the woman said, her voice rich with an accent Emily couldn't quite place.

"They are," Emily replied, snapping another photo. "It's amazing how much work goes into this."

The woman chuckled. "Oh, this is the easy part. Wait until you see the crush. That's when it gets messy."

Emily smiled and nodded, making a mental note to ask Ethan about photographing the next stage of the process.

As she moved further into the vineyard, she began to notice the personalities of the workers—each one bringing something unique to the harvest. Some sang softly as they worked, their voices blending with the hum of activity. Others exchanged stories or jokes, their laughter carrying on the breeze. It was a rhythm, a dance that seemed as old as the vineyard itself.

She paused near a cluster of workers unloading crates of freshly picked grapes onto a small trailer. A tall man with a wide-brimmed hat noticed her camera and raised an eyebrow.

"You must be the photographer Ethan mentioned," he said, setting down a crate.

"That's me," Emily said, offering a small wave. "Emily Carter."

"Luis," he said with a nod. "Welcome to the chaos. Try not to get in the way, huh?"

"Promise," Emily said with a laugh.

Luis grinned and went back to his work, but not before giving her a knowing look, as if to say, You'll see what I mean soon enough.

By midday, the pace of the harvest had quickened, and Emily found herself captivated by the seamless interplay of tradition and modernity. Wooden crates stacked high on trailers sat next to gleaming steel tanks, waiting for their load. A young woman with a ponytail was carefully testing grape samples, while an older man, perhaps one of the long-time workers, directed the sorting process with quiet authority.

Ethan appeared from behind a row of vines, carrying two steaming cups of coffee. He handed one to Emily, who took it gratefully, her fingers cold from the early autumn air.

"Getting the shots you need?" he asked.

"More than I expected," she said, gesturing to the workers. "There's so much life here. Everyone seems so connected to what they're doing."

"That's the way it should be," Ethan said, his tone thoughtful. "We've kept this a family-run operation for a reason. It's not just about making wine; it's about honoring what this land gives us and the people who bring it to life."

Emily nodded, the weight of his words sinking in. She'd photographed events and projects before, but there was something different about this. Something personal.

"Do you ever get tired of it?" she asked after a moment.

Ethan smiled faintly. "Never. It's hard work, but it's honest. Besides, every harvest is a little different. Keeps it interesting."

They stood in silence for a moment, watching as crates of grapes were loaded onto the trailer and driven toward the crush pad.

"You should come by later," Ethan said, breaking the quiet. "The crush is where the real action happens. Just be ready—it's messy, loud, and not as glamorous as the vineyard."

"I wouldn't miss it," Emily said with a grin.

As the workers began to wrap up for the day, Emily wandered back toward the main building, her memory card filled with images that told a story of labor, community, and pride. She was beginning to see what made Evergreen Estates so special—not just the land, but the people who gave it their all, year after year.

The spark in her chest flared brighter. For the first time in months, she felt like she was part of something bigger than herself.

Chapter 8

The rhythmic scrape of sandpaper filled the quiet of the boathouse as Liam worked on one of the Lady of the Lake's ribs. He had spent most of the day smoothing the wood, shaping it into something that would fit seamlessly into the skeleton of the boat. The late afternoon sun streamed through the open doors, casting long shadows across the workshop floor.

But Liam's thoughts weren't entirely on the task at hand. His mind kept wandering back to a conversation he'd had years ago with his grandfather, who had built this very boathouse.

"This lake," his grandfather had said, his voice steady but filled with emotion, "It's more than just water. It's a lifeline. A teacher. You learn from it, respect it, and it gives back.

Boats—they're the bridge between people and the water. You build one, and you're not just making something practical—you're creating something timeless, something that carries a story."

Liam had kept those words with him, even through his years in the city, where deadlines and skyscrapers had consumed his days. Now, back in the Okanagan, those words felt more significant than ever. He wasn't just restoring a boat—he was honoring those words, rebuilding a connection to the past and preserving a way of life that was slowly fading.

He set the sandpaper down and leaned against the workbench, staring at the Lady of the Lake. Her lines were graceful, even in her incomplete state, but what drew him wasn't just her physical beauty—it was the story she represented. The Okanagan had once been full of boats like her, wooden vessels that carried families, goods, and memories across the lake.

The idea had been nudging at him for weeks now, boat-building workshops.

At first, it had seemed like a far-fetched notion. Teaching others the craft would mean opening himself up, stepping out of the solitary rhythm he'd grown comfortable with. But the more he thought about it, the more it made sense. People were hungry for experiences, for a way to connect with something tangible and meaningful.

He imagined groups of people gathered in the boathouse, each working on their own small boat or learning to restore an old one. Families, friends, or even strangers coming together, hands on the wood, learning to craft something that could carry them across the water.

It would be a blend of old and new—teaching traditional methods while incorporating modern techniques and tools. A way to preserve the heritage of boat-building while ensuring it had a future.

The thought both excited and terrified him. Liam wasn't a teacher by nature, and the idea of standing in front of a group, explaining his craft, felt daunting. But he couldn't ignore the pull of it, the way the idea seemed to grow roots every time he pictured it.

The sound of footsteps on gravel pulled him from his thoughts. Ethan appeared in the doorway, holding two bottles of beer.

Liam twisted the cap off, taking a sip before smirking. "Depends—are you here to help, or just bribe me into taking a break?"

Ethan chuckled, leaning against the workbench. "Call it a little of both. Thought you could use some company."

Liam gestured around the boathouse. "Plenty of room for you to grab a tool and join in."

Ethan laughed. "I'll leave the boatbuilding to you, thanks. I've got enough on my hands with the harvest. The crew's running nonstop, but it's worth it—feels good seeing everyone working together, building something as a team."

Liam smirked. "That supposed to be your way of saying I need to stop being a hermit?"

Ethan grinned. "Maybe. Do you ever think about it? Letting people in?"

Liam hesitated, swirling the beer in his hand. "Actually, yeah. I've been thinking about running workshops. Teaching people how to build or restore boats. Something hands-on, where they could connect with the craft."

Ethan raised an eyebrow, genuinely surprised. "Seriously? That's... ambitious. But it sounds like something people would love. You've got the skills, and you'd be damn good at it, Liam."

Liam nodded, a faint smile tugging at his lips. "It's still an idea, but maybe it's time to do something bigger. Something that lasts."

Ethan clinked his bottle against Liam's. "Well, if anyone can do it, it's you. Just don't forget to save me a seat in the first workshop."

Liam shook his head, laughing softly. "Not so sure about that. I'm not exactly a people person."

"You don't have to be," Ethan said. "You just have to show them what you're passionate about. The rest will follow."

Liam glanced at the Lady of the Lake, his thoughts swirling again. "I don't know. It's a big step."

Ethan clinked his bottle against Liam's. "Big steps usually are. But they're worth it."

As Ethan left, Liam turned back to the boat, his mind still buzzing with the idea. Maybe it was time to take that step.

For now, though, he would focus on finishing the Lady of the Lake. If he could bring her back to life, maybe he could do the same for the craft itself—one boat, one workshop at a time.

Chapter 9

The drive from Kelowna to her cabin was one Emily had taken several times now, yet it never failed to unsettle her. She gripped the wheel tightly as the road twisted and turned, hugging the cliffs that dropped sharply to the lake below. The sun hung low in the sky, casting a golden glow over the water and making its surface shimmer like molten gold, but Emily barely dared to glance at it. She knew every curve by now—the tight bends, the narrow shoulders—but familiarity didn't make them feel any less precarious.

Each turn seemed designed to test her nerve, the edges unforgiving as though the asphalt had been carved reluctantly into the rugged hillside. She couldn't help but feel as if the road itself wanted her to prove she belonged there, demanding her full attention at every moment.

When she finally reached the gravel path leading to her cabin, her grip on the wheel loosened, and a shaky exhale escaped her lips. She parked and stepped out, the stillness of the evening wrapping around her like a balm. Even as she replayed the twists and turns in her mind, she couldn't deny the small rush of triumph she felt at having made it once again.

Despite the ever-present anxiety the drive inspired, the valley's beauty was undeniable. The steep cliffs, the endless lake, and the way the road seemed to dance with the land itself—it was unlike anywhere she'd ever been. The landscape felt alive, wild, and untamed, as though it was daring her to embrace its raw power. And for all its terrors, Emily couldn't help but feel a deep connection to it.

After the nerve-wracking drive back to her cabin, Emily had decided to clear her head with a walk. The path to Liam's boathouse wound through a mix of tall pines and rocky outcroppings, the lake glimmering through the trees as the sun dipped lower in the sky. By the time she reached the boathouse, a warm golden light was spilling across the water, softening the edges of the rugged landscape.

She hadn't planned on coming back so soon, but something about the quiet, deliberate energy of the place called to her, grounding her in a way few places ever had.

Liam was there, as she'd expected, bent over a section of the boat's hull, smoothing it with the practiced movements of someone who knew their craft intimately. She paused in the doorway, camera in hand, and watched for a moment. The rhythmic scrape of his tools against the wood filled the space, and the air carried the faint scent of wood shavings and varnish.

"You're back," Liam said without looking up, his voice calm and steady.

"Couldn't stay away," Emily replied, stepping inside. "There's something about this place. It feels... grounded."

Liam glanced at her briefly before returning to his work. "That's the idea. Boats like this—they're not just functional. They're pieces of history. When you work on something like this, you're connected to everything that came before."

Emily moved closer, raising her camera and snapping a few photos of his hands as they moved over the wood. "It's the same with photography," she said after a moment. "It's not just about taking pictures. It's about finding the story behind the image—capturing something real."

He straightened and looked at her, his gaze thoughtful. "And what story are you trying to tell right now?"

Emily hesitated, lowering the camera. "Honestly? I'm still figuring that out. I thought I knew, back when I had my studio in Calgary. But somewhere along the way, I lost it. Now... I'm just trying to find something that feels real again."

Liam nodded, wiping his hands on a rag. "I get that. When I was working in Vancouver, everything felt so... hollow. Deadlines, profit margins, projects that didn't mean anything. Coming back here, working with my hands— it gave me something real to hold onto."

Emily smiled faintly. "I think that's what I'm looking for. Something real to hold onto."

Liam gestured toward the boat. "You've got your camera. That's something."

She tilted her head, considering his words. "Maybe. But it's more than just the tool. It's about the process, you know? Finding the right angle, waiting for the light to hit just right. It's like... seeing the world differently, even if just for a second."

Liam leaned against the workbench, studying her. "Sounds like what I do. Except instead of light, it's wood. You've got to see the grain, the shape it wants to take. Force it too much, and you'll ruin it. Work with it, and you'll make something worth keeping."

Emily nodded, her eyes scanning the boat. "So... what's this one's story?"

"The Lady of the Lake," Liam said, his tone softening as his hand brushed the edge of the hull. "She was built in the 1920s—back when the lake was a lifeline for people here. She carried families, goods, and maybe even a few dreams. But over time, she was left behind, like so many things are. I just want to bring her back, give her another chance to be part of this place.

Emily raised her camera again, her voice quiet. "That's a beautiful sentiment. Redemption, second chances."

Liam chuckled, a rare, low sound. "Guess it is."

She snapped a few more photos, the light shifting as the sun sank lower, bathing the boathouse in hues of orange and pink.

"You ever think about what's next?" she asked, lowering the camera again.

Liam raised an eyebrow. "Next?"

"For you. For this." She gestured to the boat, the workshop.

He was quiet for a moment, his eyes on the Lady of the Lake. "I've been thinking about teaching. Workshops, maybe. Getting people involved in restoring boats like this. Passing on what I've learned."

Emily's expression brightened. "That's a great idea. People love hands-on experiences, and something like this—it's unique. You'd be preserving history while inspiring new stories."

Liam shrugged, but there was a flicker of something in his expression—hope, maybe. "It's just an idea for now. What about you? What's next for you?"

Emily hesitated, then smiled softly. "Maybe this. Telling stories like this one—through photos, capturing what makes a place or a person special. That's why I took the job with Ethan. It feels like a step in the right direction."

Liam nodded, their shared understanding settling between them.

As the last light faded from the sky, Emily gathered her things, glancing back at Liam before stepping outside.

"Thanks for letting me hang around," she said. "I'll see you soon."

"Anytime," he replied, his voice low but sincere.

As Emily walked back to her cabin, she couldn't shake the feeling that, like Liam, she was beginning to see the world—and herself—just a little differently.

Chapter 10

The boathouse was alive with the scent of freshly cut wood and the soft murmur of waves lapping against the shore. Liam stood near the Lady of the Lake, his hands brushing over her smooth, unfinished frame. Emily had returned that afternoon, drawn once again by the energy of the place and her growing curiosity about Liam's work.

Today, though, the boathouse wasn't quiet. Sitting on a stool near the open doors was Henry Sinclair, an elderly fisherman with sun-weathered skin and a glint of mischief in his eyes. His gray hair peeked out from under a battered cap, and his hands, calloused from years on the water, rested lightly on a wooden cane.

"Henry comes around now and then," Liam explained to Emily as he adjusted a clamp on the boat. "He's got stories that go back longer than anyone else I know."

Emily smiled and crouched slightly to meet the older man's gaze. "I'd love to hear them. I'm always looking for a good story."

Henry chuckled, his laughter was raspy but warm. "You want stories, eh? Well, you've come to the right place, young lady. This lake has more tales than you can count."

He motioned toward the Lady of the Lake with his cane. "She's a good name, this one. A fine name. You know where it comes from?"

Emily tilted her head. "I assumed it was something from mythology, like the Arthurian legend."

Henry waved a hand dismissively. "Oh, sure, there's that. But here in the Okanagan? The Lady of the Lake—that's our regatta queen. Back in the day, the Kelowna Regatta was the event of the summer. Boats everywhere, races, music, dances—it was the heart of the valley's social life."

Emily's interest piqued. "And the Lady of the Lake?"

"She was the star," Henry said, his eyes gleaming with nostalgia. "They'd pick a young woman from the community—a real ambassador of the Okanagan spirit. It wasn't just about looks, mind you. The Lady of the Lake had to represent the best of us—grace, charm, strength. She'd lead the parade, hand out trophies, and light up the whole regatta."

Henry leaned forward, his voice dropping conspiratorially. "You'd see her on the grand stage by the water, crowned and radiant. Everyone cheered. It was magic. That regatta brought people together, showed us what community really means."

Liam, who had been listening as he worked, paused and glanced at Henry, smiling as he asked, "And the boats? What part did they play in all this?"

"Everything," Henry said with a grin. "The regatta was built around the water. Canoe races, sailboat competitions, motorboat shows—you name it. The lake was alive back then, packed with vessels of every kind. There were parties on the water, bonfires on the shore, and laughter that echoed clear across to the other side."

Emily snapped a few photos of Henry as he spoke, her lens capturing the way his expression softened with memory. She lowered the camera and asked, "What happened to the regatta? It sounds like such an incredible tradition."

Henry's face darkened slightly, his tone losing some of its warmth. "Ah, that's the sad part of the story. It wasn't the lake or the boats that did it—it was the troublemakers. Out-of-towners, mostly, coming in for the parties. What used to be a family event turned into chaos. Riots broke out one year—storefront windows smashed, police everywhere. Next year, it was even worse. Kelowna couldn't handle it anymore, and the regatta was shut down for good."

Emily frowned. "That must've been heartbreaking for the community."

"It was," Henry said with a sigh. "You don't just lose the event—you lose the spirit it brought with it. The pride, the excitement. A lot of folks still miss it."

Liam glanced at the Lady of the Lake, his expression thoughtful. "But the name lives on."

Henry's gaze softened as he nodded. "It does. Boats like this—they carry that legacy. They remind us of the good times, what this lake meant to everyone who lived here. You're doing good work, Liam, bringing her back to life."

Emily raised her camera and snapped a photo of the older man, the boathouse, and the unfinished boat all bathed in the golden light of late afternoon. "It's amazing to think about all the stories this lake holds," she said. "Every ripple, every boat—it's all connected to something bigger."

Henry tapped his cane lightly on the floor, his voice quiet. "That's the thing about the Okanagan. You can't separate the lake from its people. It's in our blood, whether we're out on the water or just sitting here telling stories."

The three of them fell into a comfortable silence, the weight of Henry's words settling over the boathouse.

"Well," Henry said, standing slowly with a soft groan, "I've talked your ears off long enough. You two keep at it. This lake's got more stories waiting to be told."

As Henry shuffled toward the door, Emily called after him. "Thank you for sharing all of that. It means a lot."

Henry tipped his hat, his eyes twinkling. "Just don't let this one get too lost in his woodwork," he said, nodding toward Liam.

Emily laughed softly, watching him leave before turning to Liam. "Do you think the regatta could ever come back?"

Liam chuckled, shaking his head. "Who knows? Maybe it just needs the right people to believe in it again."

Chapter 11

The late afternoon sun dipped lower in the sky as Emily navigated the winding road toward Coral Beach in Lake Country, her fingers gripping the steering wheel tightly. She had asked Ethan earlier if there was a spot with a unique view of the lake, and he had mentioned this quiet stretch on the opposite side. It wasn't a tourist hotspot, he'd said, but the view across to Fintry was something special.

The road narrowed as she descended toward the lakeshore, the trees on either side thinning to reveal glimpses of water shimmering in the golden light. By the time she reached the parking area, the sun was hovering just above the hills, casting long shadows across the landscape.

Coral Beach was as peaceful as Ethan had promised. A small strip of pebbled shore stretched out before her, bordered by rocky outcroppings and a smattering of driftwood. The air was still, save for the soft lapping of the water against the shore. Across the lake, Fintry's campsite lay nestled against a backdrop of towering mountains and dense forests, all painted in shades of amber and gold by the late afternoon light. Their vivid hues shimmered on the lake's surface, broken only by the gentle ripple of the water.

Emily stepped out of her car, her camera bag slung over one shoulder. The moment her feet touched the rocky ground, she felt the quiet energy of the place—a sense of being cradled by the land and water. She pulled out her camera, adjusted the lens, and began to frame her first shot.

The light was perfect.

The sun's golden glow spilled across the lake, its rays catching on the water like liquid fire. The mountains on the Fintry side stood in sharp silhouette, their uneven outlines softened by the evening haze. Emily knelt down near the water's edge, angling her camera to capture the interplay of shadow and light.

Click.

The first shot was good, but she knew there was more to see. She moved further along the beach, pausing to frame driftwood against the backdrop of the mountains. Her lens captured every detail—the texture of the weathered wood, the sparkling dance of light on the waves, and the serene majesty of the landscape.

Click. Click.

Emily felt a thrill she hadn't experienced in months. It wasn't just about taking pictures—it was about finding the right moment, the one where the world seemed to hold its breath, offering something fleeting and perfect.

As the sun slipped over the mountain, painting the sky in hues of orange, pink, and violet, Emily climbed onto a large boulder at the edge of the shore. From this vantage point, she could see for miles down the lake, stretching out like a mirror reflecting the sky's fire. She adjusted her settings, taking a deep breath to steady herself before pressing the shutter again.

Click.

The shot was breathtaking. The lake glowed like molten gold, with the silhouette of Fintry's mountains standing proud against the vibrant sky. She could almost feel the stories this place held, the connection between the land and the people who called it home.

Emily lowered her camera and sat for a moment, her feet dangling just above the water. For the first time in what felt like forever, she wasn't thinking about the past or worrying about the future. She was simply present, immersed in the beauty of the world around her.

Her camera rested in her lap, warm from the day's work, and her mind buzzed with ideas. She could see a series taking shape—images that told the story of this lake and its people, of the life and history that flowed through these waters.

The sun dipped below the horizon, leaving behind a deep, fiery glow that faded into soft indigos and silvers. Emily stood, brushing off her jeans, and slung her camera over her shoulder. The quiet stillness of Coral Beach seemed to echo in her heart as she made her way back to the car.

Driving back along the winding road, she glanced in her rearview mirror at the fading light over the lake. Her artistic spark wasn't just reignited—it was blazing, fueled by the raw, unfiltered beauty of the Okanagan.

For the first time in a long while, Emily felt alive.

Chapter 12

The scent of roasted chestnuts and fresh baked goods filled the air as Emily wandered through the Artisan Fair in downtown Kelowna. The park was alive with activity—vendors displaying handmade crafts, artists sketching, and local farmers showcasing the season's best produce. String lights crisscrossed above the booths, and the cheerful hum of conversation mingled with the strumming of a guitarist at the far end of the fair.

Emily had come to capture the atmosphere, her camera swinging lightly from her neck. The fair was a photographer's dream, bursting with color and character. She stopped at a booth selling hand-carved wooden ornaments, snapping photos of the craftsman's gnarled hands as he worked. Nearby, children crowded around a table of homemade fudge, their laughter ringing out over the soft hum of activity.

As she turned to frame another shot, a familiar voice called out, rough but warm.

"Miss Photographer! Fancy seeing you here."

Emily turned and smiled, spotting Henry sitting on a bench near a stall selling homemade preserves. He wore the same battered cap, his weathered hands wrapped around a steaming cup of cider.

"Henry!" she said, making her way over. "I didn't expect to see you here."

"Ah, these old legs don't get me around much anymore, but I couldn't miss the fair," he said, patting the bench beside him. "Come, sit. This place has more stories than the lake itself."

Emily sat down, the energy of the fair buzzing around them. "Stories, huh? What's the best one you've got about this area?"

Henry chuckled, his eyes twinkling. "Oh, you young folks don't even know the half of it. This place, right over there in City Park? It was once home to the old Kelowna Aquatic Centre. Had a massive building, a diving tower, and even a stadium. Back in its day, it was something to see."

Emily raised an eyebrow. "An aquatic center? Here?"

"Oh, yes," Henry said, nodding. "The center was the heart of this city for years. Summers were spent swimming, diving, and just lounging by the water. You couldn't find a livelier spot in all of Kelowna."

He took a sip of his coffee, then leaned forward, lowering his voice slightly. "My brother and I would go swimming there. One time, when we were teenagers, he decided he was gonna jump off the top of the diving tower. I told him he was crazy, but he did it anyway."

Henry paused, shaking his head with a wry grin. "A guy jumped off too soon and landed right on him. Broke his arm. He tried to keep it quiet, but Mom knew the moment we got home. She was furious. Still, he'd tell you it was worth it—said that jump made him a legend for a whole summer."

Emily laughed softly, imagining the scene. "That sounds... chaotic. And dangerous."

"Ah, it was a different time," Henry said with a shrug. "But it wasn't just for the locals. People came from all over to see the diving competitions and the swimming races. It brought everyone together."

"So, what happened to it?" Emily asked, leaning forward.

Henry's face grew more serious. "The center and the grandstands burned down in 1969. One night, there was a fire—it gutted the whole thing. Never did find out how it started. The city decided not to rebuild. Broke a lot of hearts, losing that place. The diving tower stayed standing for a while, but they took it down in 1980."

He gestured around the park with his cane. "Now it's just memories. This fair, the music, the laughter—it reminds me of those days. Feels like a little piece of it is still here."

Emily glanced around, her eyes lingering on the joyful faces and vibrant energy of the fair. She raised her camera and framed a shot of the scene before her—families strolling through the rows of stalls, the lights casting a warm glow, and the mountains standing tall in the background.

"You're right," she said quietly. "There's something special about this place. It feels... timeless."

Henry smiled, his gaze distant. "That's Kelowna for you. It's always changing, but it never really loses its heart."

They sat in companionable silence for a moment before Henry turned to her with a wink. "You're good at finding stories, Miss

Photographer. Don't forget to tell your own along the way."

Emily smiled, the weight of his words settling over her. She lifted her camera again, capturing the moment—the man with his cup of cider, the twinkling lights of the fair, and the enduring spirit of a place that held so much history.

As the sun dipped below the horizon and the fair lights began to glow, Emily felt a quiet connection—not just to Henry's stories, but to the Okanagan itself. It stirred memories of her visits to the valley when her parents lived here, the familiarity of the landscape mingling with the new stories she was discovering.

Chapter 13

The rhythmic hum of machinery and the lively chatter of workers greeted Emily as she approached the crush pad at Evergreen Estates. The air was thick with the pungent aroma of crushed grapes, a heady mixture of sweetness and fermentation that spoke to the heart of winemaking.

Ethan stood at the center of it all, directing his team with calm efficiency. He wore a baseball cap pulled low over his dark hair, and his shirt sleeves were rolled up to his elbows, revealing forearms stained with grape juice. He spotted Emily as she approached, raising a hand in greeting.

"Perfect timing," he said, his voice cutting through the hum of activity. "This is where the magic begins—or the mess, depending on how you look at it."

Emily laughed, adjusting the strap of her camera. "I'll try not to get in the way. But I definitely want to capture this."

Ethan gestured toward the workers pouring crates of freshly picked grapes into the de-stemmer, the fruit tumbling in a cascade of deep purples and reds. "It's controlled chaos, but it's the heartbeat of the harvest. You can feel the energy here—it's what keeps this place alive."

Emily moved closer, carefully framing a shot of the grapes as they were funneled into the crusher. The machine's whirring sound was almost meditative, punctuated by the occasional shout or laugh from the workers. She snapped photo after photo, capturing the vibrant colors, the movement, and the camaraderie among the team.

One worker, a young woman with her hair pulled into a loose braid, caught Emily's attention. She was laughing as she wiped her hands on her jeans, her face streaked with juice. Emily quickly raised her camera, capturing the moment of pure joy and connection to the work.

Ethan appeared beside her, leaning slightly to see the shot on her camera's screen. "That's a good one," he said. "It's not just about the process—it's about the people. That's what makes this place special."

Emily nodded, her fingers adjusting the lens to focus on a worker carefully sampling juice from a spout, the intensity of his expression illuminated by the golden afternoon light. "You can feel the pride here. It's not just a job—it's part of something bigger."

"That's the idea," Ethan said, his voice tinged with quiet pride. "My parents taught me that early on. Wine isn't just a product—it's a story. Every bottle carries a piece of this land, these people, this moment."

As the afternoon wore on, Emily moved around the crush pad, her camera capturing the details of the process—the grape-stained hands, the intricate machinery, the way sunlight caught on the cascading juice as it flowed into stainless steel tanks.

Ethan occasionally stopped to explain what was happening, describing the balance between science and art that defined winemaking. His passion for the craft was evident in every word, and Emily couldn't help but feel inspired by his dedication.

By the time the sun began to dip below the horizon, casting long shadows across the vineyard, Emily's memory card was nearly full.

She lowered her camera and turned to Ethan, a small smile tugging at her lips.

"Thank you for letting me be part of this," she said. "I think I captured something special today."

Ethan smiled back, tipping his cap. "You've got a good eye. I can't wait to see the finished shots."

As she drove back to her cabin that evening, Emily couldn't stop thinking about the day's events. The energy, the connection, the sense of purpose—it all reminded her why she had picked up a camera in the first place.

She parked and stepped out into the cool night air, pausing to glance at the lake glittering under the moonlight. Tomorrow, she would sort through the photos, reliving each moment through her lens.

For now, she let herself savor the feeling of belonging, of being part of something meaningful again.

Chapter 14

The buzz of lively conversation filled the old Okanagan Mission Community Hall as people milled around tables displaying everything from vintage furniture to handmade quilts. The annual charity auction was in full swing, a much-anticipated event that brought together locals and visitors to support a community youth program. Liam had never been much of an auction enthusiast, but the event had drawn his curiosity—along with a promise to Ethan to show up and bid on a bottle of rare wine for Evergreen Estates.

Liam stood at the back of the room, his hands shoved into his pockets, casually surveying the items up for bidding. The hum of friendly chatter and the warm scent of coffee brewing in a corner reminded him of simpler days. He hadn't planned to buy anything, but one item in particular caught his eye—a wooden model of a boat, displayed on a small table near the stage.

It wasn't just any model. The craftsmanship was meticulous, with tiny, intricate details etched into its hull and sails. The base had been worn smooth by time, but there was something undeniably familiar about the design. Liam moved closer, his eyes narrowing as he studied the curves of the miniature hull.

"That's an old one," a voice said beside him.

Liam turned to see an elderly man standing nearby. His hair was long and silver, tied neatly at the nape of his neck, and his eyes carried a quiet wisdom. Liam recognized him—Sammy, a respected Syilx elder who had shared his knowledge of local history at various community events.

"Looks like it," Liam replied, gesturing to the model. "Any idea where it's from?"

Sammy stepped closer, his expression shifting as he studied the boat. He reached out, running his fingers lightly over the weathered wood. "This is the work of a Syilx," he said softly. "Hand-carved. It's been passed down, I'd wager. A piece like this isn't made to be sold."

Liam frowned, intrigued. "How did it end up here, then?"

Sammy shook his head. "Hard to say. Could've been gifted, lost, or even taken. But I can tell you this—whoever made it, they knew this lake well. Look at the lines. That's Okanagan Lake carved into the hull. And here—" He pointed to a small engraving on the base. "That's a family mark. This boat carries a story."

The auctioneer's voice boomed over the room, announcing the start of bidding for the next item: the model boat. Liam hesitated, glancing between Sammy and the artifact.

"You should have it," Sammy said quietly. "Something like this belongs to someone who understands its value. And I think you do."

The bidding began, and Liam raised his hand without overthinking it. A few others placed bids, but he stayed in, raising the stakes each time. Finally, after what felt like an eternity, the gavel struck, and the auctioneer declared him the winner.

The room broke into polite applause, but Liam barely noticed. He stepped forward to collect the model, its weight solid and reassuring in his hands. Sammy approached him again, his expression unreadable.

"Good," the elder said simply. "Now it's yours to protect."

Emily arrived at the auction late, her camera slung over her shoulder. She spotted Liam near the corner, holding the boat and speaking with Sammy. Curious, she approached, her footsteps soft against the worn wooden floor.

"What's this?" she asked, her gaze falling to the model in Liam's hands.

"It's an old Syilx boat model," Liam explained. "Sammy says it's got a history—something tied to the lake."

Sammy nodded. "That's right. This was likely carved by someone who lived by these waters long ago. You can tell from the detail—it's more than just a toy. It's a map of the lake and a piece of our culture."

Emily raised her camera, glancing at Sammy for permission before snapping a photo of the artifact in Liam's hands. "That's incredible. What do you plan to do with it?"

Liam hesitated. "Not sure yet. But I want to learn more about where it came from."

Sammy smiled faintly. "The story will reveal itself in time, if you're patient."

Emily watched as Liam studied the boat, a mixture of awe and determination in his expression. She snapped another photo, capturing the moment—a craftsman holding a piece of history, and an elder guiding its future.

Before they could leave, Ethan's familiar voice cut through the din of the auction hall. "What did you find, Liam?"

Emily turned to see Ethan approaching, a wine bottle cradled under one arm and an amused smile on his face. His casual demeanor stood out against the lively chaos of the crowd.

Liam smirked. "Ethan. You're late—I already outbid you on the interesting stuff."

Ethan laughed, nodding toward the model in Liam's hands. "So you're the one who snagged the boat model. Looks like you've got a new project."

"More like a new mystery," Liam replied, his tone lighter than usual. "Sammy says it's Syilx work. Something worth digging into."

Ethan's brow furrowed as he stepped closer to inspect the model. "Sammy's usually right about these things. If he says it's special, it probably is."

Emily lifted her camera slightly, capturing a candid shot of the two men as they examined the artifact, their expressions marked by curiosity and respect for its history.

Ethan glanced at her, catching the motion. "You're everywhere with that thing, aren't you?"

"Always," Emily replied with a grin. "Moments like this don't wait."

Ethan nodded, a flicker of admiration crossing his face. "Fair enough. Just make sure to save some shots for the vineyard. I've got some new barrels coming in next week— might make for good material."

"I'll be there," Emily promised, sliding the camera strap higher on her shoulder.

Ethan patted Liam on the shoulder. "Let me know what you find out about that boat. I've got a feeling it's worth more than just what you paid for it."

As Ethan headed toward the exit, Liam turned back to Emily, his grip on the model tightening slightly.

As they left the auction together, Emily couldn't help but feel that the artifact wasn't just a relic of the past—it was a thread connecting Liam to something much larger than himself.

Chapter 15

Emily arrived at the boathouse just as the sun began its slow descent, casting long shadows across the lake. The rhythmic scrape of sandpaper greeted her as she stepped inside, her eyes adjusting to the warm light filtering through the open doors. Liam was at his usual place, smoothing out a plank for the Lady of the Lake.

But today, he wasn't alone. Henry sat nearby on a folding chair, his cane resting against the workbench. Ethan leaned casually against the far wall, a bottle of beer in hand, his expression relaxed but curious as he listened to Henry recount a tale.

"Emily," Liam greeted, glancing up briefly from his work. "Didn't expect you today."

"Couldn't resist," she replied with a smile. "What's the story?"

Henry turned toward her, his eyes glinting with mischief and something darker. "You picked a good time to show up, young lady. I was just about to tell these lads a tale—a bit of local history with a sinister twist."

Emily took a seat on a nearby stool, setting her camera on her lap. "I'm all ears."

Henry leaned forward slightly, his weathered hands resting on his knees. "This one's about the old railroad. Back when Kelowna had its tracks running through, there was a man—a friend of my dad's—worked for the railroad his whole life. Hard worker, quiet type. At 55, he was still on the job, but one day, just like that, he was gone."

"Gone how?" Ethan asked, his tone skeptical but intrigued.

They said he drowned," Henry replied, his voice dropping slightly. "Fishing near the old boom docks on Westside Road. You know, those piles of logs chained together, floating in the water, waiting to be sent to the mill. But here's the thing—he wasn't a fisherman. Never once in his life did he pick up a rod."

Emily frowned. "So what happened?"

"That's the question, isn't it?" Henry said, shaking his head. "They found his body tangled in fishing line, washed up on the shore. Looked like an accident, but there were whispers—rumors about how he might've gotten mixed up in something he shouldn't have."

Liam paused in his sanding, his expression darkening. "Like what?"

Henry's lips curled into a grim smile. "Opium. Back then, the railroad wasn't just moving goods and people. There were... other things riding those trains. Things that folks weren't supposed to know about. My dad's friend—he'd been seen hanging around the wrong crowds, staying late after shifts."

Ethan crossed his arms, his brow furrowed. "That doesn't mean anything. A lot of people worked late shifts."

Henry nodded. "True. But a few years after he died, his family found something— something that made them question everything."

"What did they find?" Emily asked, her voice barely above a whisper.

"A little black book," Henry said, his tone ominous. "Names, numbers, and notes in it. Nobody knew what it meant, but when they called one of the numbers, they were told in no uncertain terms to burn the book. 'Or else,' they said."

"Or else what?" Liam asked, his jaw tightening.

Henry shrugged. "Guess they didn't want to find out. The family burned it, and that was the end of it—or so they thought. For years, strange things kept happening—accidents, fires, even another drowning in the same spot."

Ethan rubbed the back of his neck. "You're saying someone was tied to this guy's death. Someone who didn't want whatever he knew getting out?"

"That's exactly what I'm saying," Henry replied. "The railroad was more than just a business back then. It was a lifeline for smugglers, criminals, and folks who didn't mind getting their hands dirty."

Emily sat back, her mind racing. "Do you think his death was an accident?"

Henry's gaze drifted toward the lake, his expression distant. "Some say it was. Others... well, you don't drown yourself in fishing line when you've never fished a day in your life."

The room fell silent, the weight of the story settling over them like a heavy fog. Outside, the lake glimmered softly in the fading light, its stillness belying the darkness Henry had just described.

"Well," Henry said finally, breaking the silence. "That's enough of the past for one day. This old man needs a drink."

He stood slowly, leaning on his cane as he made his way toward the door. "Remember, kids," he added with a wry grin, "Not all stories have happy endings."

As Henry disappeared into the evening light, Emily glanced at Ethan and Liam, their expressions unreadable.

"You think there's any truth to that?" she asked, breaking the quiet.

Ethan shrugged, his face still thoughtful. "Who knows? But Henry's not the type to make things up."

Liam nodded, his eyes lingering on the Lady of the Lake. "Stories like that—they stick for a reason. Might be worth digging into someday."

Emily raised her camera, snapping a photo of the boat framed against the twilight sky. "This lake keeps surprising me," she said softly.

Liam glanced at her, his expression lightening just slightly. "Welcome to the Okanagan."

Chapter 16

The idea came to Emily as she sat by the lake later that evening, her camera resting on her lap. The stories she had heard—from Henry's dark tale of the railroad to the rich histories woven through the Lady of the Lake and the Kelowna Regatta—played on repeat in her mind. The Okanagan wasn't just beautiful, it was alive with untold stories, threads of the past and present intertwined in ways she had never considered.

She raised her camera and framed the scene before her. The lake was calm, its surface reflecting the deep hues of twilight. Across the water, Coral Beach stood in quiet majesty, it's rugged edges softened by the fading light. She snapped the photo, knowing it would be the first of many.

"Under the Okanagan Sun," she whispered to herself, the words slipping out as if they had been waiting for her to speak them.

The phrase felt right—like it belonged to the land as much as the stories she wanted to capture through her camera.

The next morning, Emily sat at her desk in the cabin, sorting through her recent photos. Images of the vineyard's harvest, the chaos of the crush pad, the artisans at the fair, and Liam working on the Lady of the Lake filled her screen. Each one told a story, but together, they felt incomplete—like pieces of a puzzle waiting to come together.

She began organizing them, grouping them by theme, people, land, and history. Her fingers hovered over the keyboard as she typed out the title for a new folder: *Under the Okanagan Sun: A Photo Series.*

Her vision started to take shape. The series would go beyond the surface beauty of the valley, delving into its untold stories—the fishermen who had worked these waters, the farmers who had tended the land, the craftspeople who had left their mark. She wanted to honor the past while celebrating the present, creating a tapestry of images that reflected the Okanagan's essence.

Later that day, she returned to Evergreen Estates, eager to add to her growing collection. Ethan greeted her with a nod as she wandered through the vineyard, her camera ready.

"You're back," he said, pausing from his work.

"I'm starting a new series," Emily replied, her eyes scanning the vines. "I want to tell the story of this place—not just the vineyard, but the people, the land, the history."

Ethan smiled faintly. "Sounds ambitious."

"It is," she admitted, raising her camera to capture the golden light filtering through the grape leaves. "But this valley deserves it. There's so much here that people don't see, don't even think about."

"Well," Ethan said, leaning on a post, "if anyone can do it, it's you. Just let me know if you need more stories—or wine."

Emily laughed softly and continued her work, the rhythm of the vineyard settling into her bones.

Over the next few weeks, her project began to take shape. She revisited Liam at the boathouse, capturing his steady hands as they restored the Lady of the Lake. She found Henry again, this time at a small dock, staring out at the water with a wistful smile. She followed the roads winding through the valley, photographing the orchards, the old train tracks, and the quiet corners where the land seemed to hold its breath.

Every shot felt like a piece of the puzzle falling into place. The photo series wasn't just a project—it was a journey, a way for Emily to reconnect with herself and her craft.

One evening, as she reviewed her latest shots, she couldn't help but feel a spark of pride. The images captured something deeper than scenery, they told the story of a place shaped by its people, history, and enduring spirit.

The Okanagan wasn't just a setting—it was a character, alive and pulsing with life under the sun.

Chapter 17

The calm, glassy surface of Okanagan Lake betrayed none of the turmoil brewing around it. For weeks, tension had been building in the community as whispers about the developments along the lakeshore circulated. Proposals for luxury resorts, expanded marinas, and even private docks had divided the valley. To some, it was progress—a chance to bring in tourists and revitalize the local economy. To others, it was a threat to the lake's fragile ecosystem and the way of life they held dear.

Emily heard the arguments as she wandered through the farmer's market that morning, her camera slung over her shoulder. A small group of locals had gathered near the coffee stand, their voices rising as the discussion grew heated.

"It's not right!" an older woman said, her hands on her hips. "We've spent decades protecting this lake, and now they want to turn it into a playground for the rich?"

"It's not like that," a younger man countered, his face flushed. "The tourism dollars could help everyone, especially the small businesses. Don't you want the valley to thrive?"

"I want the lake to survive," the woman shot back. "What good is thriving if we destroy what makes this place special?"

Emily lingered at the edge of the crowd, snapping a few discreet photos of the scene. The emotions etched into their faces told a story in themselves—one of a community caught between preserving its roots and embracing change.

Later that day, she stopped by Liam's boathouse to share the photos and see if he had heard about the controversy. She found him working on the Lady of the Lake, his usual quiet focus replaced by a tension she hadn't seen before.

"You okay?" she asked, leaning against the doorframe.

Liam sighed, setting down his tool. "You've heard about the marina expansion plans, haven't you?"

Emily nodded. "It's all anyone's talking about at the market. Are you involved?"

"Not directly," Liam said, wiping his hands on a rag. "But it's hard not to be. People are divided. Some think it'll bring opportunities. Others think it'll destroy everything. I can see both sides, but... I don't know. The lake's not just a resource. It's part of who we are."

Ethan arrived a few minutes later, his expression as dark as Liam's. "You won't believe this," he said, stepping into the boathouse. "The developers are pushing for an emergency town hall meeting next week. They're trying to fast-track approvals for the marina project."

Liam's jaw tightened. "Figures. They're not interested in what the locals think—they just want their permits."

Emily stayed quiet, sensing the weight of the issue on both men. Ethan leaned against the workbench, shaking his head.

"I'm all for tourism," he said, "But this isn't the way to do it. Evergreen relies on the lake, just like a lot of the small businesses here. If they overbuild, they'll ruin the balance. And if the lake suffers, we all do."

"They don't care about balance," Liam said bitterly. "They care about profits."

Emily raised her camera, snapping a shot of the two men deep in conversation, their frustration clear. "What are you going to do?" she asked.

Ethan glanced at her, his brow furrowed. "We're going to the meeting. People need to speak up. This isn't just about a few businesses or some tourists—it's about what kind of place we want this valley to be."

Liam nodded, his expression grim but resolute. "The lake has been here long before any of us. It deserves a voice too."

Emily felt a surge of admiration for both men. They weren't just talking—they were ready to act. She realized that her photo series, Under the Okanagan Sun, could be a way to amplify their message. The stories she captured could show what was at stake—not just the beauty of the lake, but the lives and traditions it sustained.

"I'll be there," she said, her voice firm. "With my camera. People need to see what's worth fighting for."

The three of them stood in silence for a moment, the light from the setting sun streaming through the open doors of the boathouse. Outside, the lake lay still, its serene surface hiding the undercurrents of change and conflict.

For Emily, it wasn't just about taking pictures anymore. It was about capturing a story that mattered—and making sure it was told.

Liam broke the silence first, his voice quiet but carrying a note of reflection. "She's so much like Claire."

Emily turned, curious. "Claire? Who's that?"

Ethan smiled faintly, his expression softening at the mention of the name. "Claire Bennett. She's a travel writer. She wrote a piece on wineries in Okanagan last year. It wasn't just about the wine, though. It was about the land, the people, and the stories behind it all."

"She didn't just write about us," Liam added, leaning against the workbench. "She dug deeper—wanted to understand why we do what we do. She had a way of seeing things most people overlook. You remind me of her."

Emily felt a flicker of both pride and pressure at the comparison. "She sounds amazing. Did you know her well?"

Ethan nodded, his gaze distant. "I did. She stayed in the valley for a while—long enough to leave an impression. Claire's the reason a lot of people started looking at this place differently. She showed how special it really is."

"She left something behind," Liam said, his voice softer now. "Not just her story, but the way she made people see the Okanagan. You have that same spark. That drive to tell the truth, not just what's easy or pretty."

Emily felt the weight of their words, but it wasn't unwelcome. Instead, it lit a fire inside her—a determination to live up to the legacy of someone like Claire Bennett, to tell stories that would resonate long after the final photo was taken.

"I'd love to read her article," Emily said, looking between the two men. "If it's anything like what you've said, I bet it's incredible."

"I've got a copy back at the vineyard," Ethan offered. "I'll show it to you next time I see you."

"Thanks," Emily said, her voice quiet but firm. "I'd like to see how she brought this place to life."

For a moment, none of them spoke, the air thick with unspoken thoughts. Outside, the lake's stillness mirrored the weight of the conversation—a calm surface hiding the ripples of shared memories and the growing connections between them

Chapter 18

The air was heavy with the smell of rain as dark clouds gathered over the Okanagan Valley. Emily had been working late, sorting through her photos at the cabin, when the first crack of thunder rolled across the lake. She glanced out the window, watching as the trees swayed under the growing force of the wind.

A sudden pang of worry struck her—Liam's boathouse.

She grabbed her jacket and camera bag, throwing them over her shoulder before heading out into the storm. The walk to Liam's was treacherous—the rain poured in relentless sheets, and the narrow path seemed to disappear beneath the downpour. Lightning lit up the sky, illuminating the lake in flashes of eerie brilliance.

When she finally arrived, the scene took her breath away. Waves crashed violently against the shoreline, and the wind howled through the open doors of the boathouse. The structure groaned under the strain, its weathered cedar siding no match for the fury of the storm.

"Liam!" Emily shouted, running toward the boathouse. Her voice barely carried over the roar of the wind and rain.

Inside, she found Liam bracing a tarp against the boat, his hair and clothes soaked through. He looked up as she entered, his face a mixture of relief and frustration.

"Emily! What are you doing here?" he yelled, tying the tarp down with a rope.

"I was worried!" she shouted back, stepping forward to help him secure the covering. "This storm is insane!"

The wind picked up, slamming the doors against the frame with a deafening crash. Liam winced but didn't stop working. Together, they managed to fasten the tarp over the Lady of the Lake, shielding her from the worst of the rain.

But the damage had already started. A section of the roof had caved in, and water was pouring onto the workbench below.

Tools and wood scraps floated in shallow pools on the floor.

"I can't hold it together," Liam said, his voice tight with frustration. "This place wasn't built for a storm like this."

Emily placed a hand on his arm, her grip firm. "What can I do?"

By morning, the storm had passed, leaving the valley drenched and eerily quiet. The boathouse, however, was in bad shape. The roof sagged in places, and the floor was littered with debris. The Lady of the Lake had survived, but the damage around her was unmistakable.

Word spread quickly, and by midday, members of the community began to show up. Ethan arrived first, carrying a toolbox and a determined expression.

"You're not fixing this alone," he said firmly, clapping a hand on Liam's shoulder.

Henry showed up next, leaning on his cane but ready to offer advice. A few neighbors followed, armed with tools, tarps, and spare lumber.

"Looks like you've got quite the crew," Emily said, smiling at Liam as she snapped a photo of the impromptu gathering.

Liam looked around, his usual stoicism softened by gratitude. "Guess I underestimated this place."

The work was hard, but the collective effort brought the boathouse back to life piece by piece. As the sun began to set, casting golden light over the lake, the repairs were nearly complete.

Emily captured the scene with her camera—the sweat-soaked shirts, the laughter and determination, the way the community came together in the face of adversity.

"This isn't just a boathouse," Ethan said quietly, standing beside her. "It's a symbol. Of what this valley stands for—resilience, connection, and people who look out for each other."

Emily nodded, her heart full as she framed the final shot. Liam, surrounded by his neighbors, stood with his hand resting on the Lady of the Lake. The boathouse, though battered, stood tall once more—a testament to the strength of the community and the enduring spirit of the lake.

As the evening settled in and the group began to disperse, Liam turned to Emily, his expression uncharacteristically soft. "Thanks for being here. I mean it."

Emily smiled. "Happy to help."

He held her gaze for a moment before glancing away, his hand trailing gently along the boat's hull. "Maybe this storm wasn't all bad. Sometimes, it takes a little chaos to reveal what's worth rebuilding."

Emily snapped one last photo, the golden light fading behind the hills. The storm had left its mark, but so had the people who weathered it together.

Chapter 19

The morning light streamed through the cabin's old wooden shutters, casting soft patterns across the floor. Emily sat at the small kitchen table, sipping her coffee and sorting through her photos from the previous day. The images were good—some of her best, she thought—but her focus kept drifting to the sense of history that seemed to linger in every corner of the valley.

She glanced at the far corner of the cabin, where a loose floorboard had caught her attention the night before. It had been too late to investigate, but now, in the quiet stillness of the morning, curiosity tugged at her.

Setting her coffee down, Emily grabbed a screwdriver and knelt beside the board. The wood creaked as she pried it up, revealing a small hollow space beneath. Her breath caught when she spotted something wrapped in faded fabric—a bundle that looked untouched for decades.

Carefully, she pulled it out and unwrapped the fabric, her fingers trembling slightly. Inside were several folded letters, their edges yellowed with age. The paper was fragile, and the ink was faint but still legible. Her heart raced as she unfolded the first one, her eyes scanning the neat, looping handwriting.

January 20th, 1903
My Dearest Anna,
The days grow longer without you, and I feel the weight of every hour we are apart. The world may see us as wrong, but my heart knows the truth—we were meant to find each other in this wild and untamed land. Every time I see the lake, I think of the moments we've stolen together and the future we dreamed of, despite the odds.
Yours always, James.

Emily's brow furrowed as she read the letter again, her mind spinning with questions. James and Anna. Who were they? What had brought them together, and what had kept them apart?

She set the letter aside and opened another. This one was shorter, more urgent.

February 08th, 1901
Anna,
I fear my father has learned of us. He speaks of sending me away, to the city or even back East. I cannot let him tear us apart. Meet me by the old cedar grove at dusk. If we must leave this place to be together, so be it. I will not let anyone decide our fate but us.
Forever yours, James.

A shiver ran through Emily as she pieced the story together. This wasn't just a simple romance—it was something more complicated, something forbidden. She felt the weight of the letters in her hands, as though they carried not just words but the emotions of lives long past.

She read through the rest of the letters, each one revealing more of the story. James, the son of a settler family, and Anna, a young Syilx woman, had fallen in love despite the barriers that society—and their families—had placed between them. Their words spoke of secret meetings by the lake, plans to escape, and the deep connection they shared.

One letter, however, stopped Emily cold. It was the last in the bundle, and it carried a sense of finality that the others did not.

November 28th, 1902
Anna,
I waited at the cedar grove, but you never came. The stars have long since risen, and still, I stand here, hoping, praying. My father has promised terrible things if I do not return tonight, but I cannot leave without knowing you are safe. If you read this, please find me. We will find a way, no matter what stands in our path.
Yours, now and always, James.

The date on the letter was over a century old. Emily's chest tightened as she imagined James waiting by the grove, his hope dwindling with each passing moment. Had Anna ever reached him? Or had their love story ended in heartbreak?

She leaned back against the wall, staring at the letters spread out before her. These weren't just pieces of paper—they were windows into a world that felt both distant and achingly close. The love they described was raw and real, and the pain of their separation lingered like a ghost in the air.

Emily carefully gathered the letters, placed them back into the fabric, and tucked them into her camera bag. She couldn't leave them behind, not when they felt so connected to the valley she was starting to call home.

She made a silent promise to herself as she zipped the bag shut, she would find out what had happened to James and Anna. Their story deserved to be told, not forgotten in the shadows of an old cabin.

Chapter 20

The letters weighed heavily in Emily's bag as she approached Liam's boathouse the next morning. The sun had just begun its ascent, casting a soft light over the lake, but her mind was fixed on the questions that had kept her awake half the night. Who were James and Anna? And why had their story been hidden for so long?

Liam was already at work when she arrived, smoothing a plank for the Lady of the Lake. He looked up as she stepped inside, his expression curious.

"You're here early," he said, setting the plank aside.

"I need your help," Emily said without preamble, pulling the bundle of letters from her bag and unwrapping them. She handed the first one to Liam, who studied it carefully, his brow furrowing as he read.

"James and Anna," he murmured. "Sounds like they had a rough time of it."

"They weren't just any couple," Emily explained. "James was a settler, and Anna was Syilx. They had to keep their relationship a secret, and these letters are all that's left of their story. I need to know more."

Liam nodded, handing the letter back. "I might know someone who can help. Sammy, the elder who told me about the boat model, has a deep knowledge of local history. If anyone can piece this together, it's him."

A few hours later, Emily and Liam sat on a bench outside a modest house near the edge of the reserve. Sammy greeted them with a warm smile, his sharp eyes taking in the letters Emily held and the boat model Liam carried.

"Well," Sammy said, gesturing for them to sit under the shade of a cedar tree in his yard. "What brings you two here?"

Emily carefully unfolded one of the letters and placed it on the table between them. "I found these in my cabin. They tell the story of James and Anna—a settler and a Syilx woman. I was hoping you might know something about them."

Sammy's gaze lingered on the letter, his expression growing thoughtful. "Anna. That name's familiar. There was a story passed down in my family about a woman who fell in love with someone she wasn't supposed to. Caused quite a stir back in the day."

Liam set the boat model beside the letter. "We were also hoping you could tell us more about this. You mentioned it was Syilx work, and we're trying to understand its connection to the lake."

Sammy picked up the model, his fingers tracing the intricate carvings. "This was made by a master carver, no doubt about it. The markings on the hull—they're a map of the lake. Each one of these etchings represents a significant place, likely tied to fishing or gathering sites."

He turned the model over, revealing a faint engraving on the base. "This here? It's a family mark. I'd bet this belonged to someone important—a chief, maybe, or a respected elder."

Emily leaned forward, her voice hesitant. "Do you think it could be connected to Anna's story?"

Sammy's eyes softened as he considered the question. "It's possible. Our stories are like the lake—they flow into one another, each one shaping the next. If James and Anna were tied to this place, their lives would've touched many others."

He picked up the letter again, his voice quieter now. "Anna's story is one of love and loss, but also resistance. To love outside of what was accepted—especially then—took great courage. It's no surprise their story was hidden. Many families kept secrets like this to protect their own."

Liam nodded, his expression serious. "And the boat?"

Sammy smiled faintly. "It's a symbol of connection—between the land and the water, the past and the present. Whoever made this wanted to preserve something important. It's no coincidence it's found its way to you."

Emily felt a chill run through her as Sammy's words sank in. The lake, the letters, the boat—they weren't just random pieces of history. They were threads of a story waiting to be woven together.

"What do we do now?" she asked, her voice steady despite the emotions swirling inside her.

Sammy placed the boat model gently on the table. "You honor the story. You share it. The past isn't meant to be forgotten—it's meant to guide us."

As they left Sammy's house, Emily couldn't shake the feeling that she and Liam were part of something larger than themselves. The lake, the letters, the boat—they were all connected, their stories flowing together like tributaries feeding into the same vast body of water.

For the first time, Emily felt certain that her photo series, *Under the Okanagan Sun*, was about more than just the beauty of the valley.

Chapter 21

The morning light filtering through the boathouse windows created a soft glow, illuminating the Lady of the Lake as if the boat itself held a quiet magic. Emily adjusted her camera settings, and the steady rhythm of Liam's sanding provided a calming soundtrack. She'd been coming here more frequently now, capturing the slow transformation of the boat, the deliberate care of Liam's hands, and the way the wood seemed to come alive under his touch.

Her mornings were split these days—early hours spent photographing Ethan's harvest and winemaking process, then late afternoons at the boathouse. Ethan had been pleased with her work so far, even suggesting a few of the shots might be used in next year's winery promotions. But there was something different about Liam's work that pulled her back again and again. It wasn't for a paycheck. It wasn't for anyone else's agenda. It was pure dedication—something personal.

"You know you don't have to keep coming back," Liam said suddenly, his voice breaking through her focus.

Emily lowered her camera, peering at him over the lens. "And miss this? Not a chance."

Liam shook his head but didn't argue, his faint smile betraying his amusement. "I'm not that interesting."

"Maybe not to you," Emily replied, "But to my camera, you are."

She moved closer, crouching to capture the texture of the wood grain, the faint markings that still lingered from the boat's past. Liam had taken to working with the doors of the boathouse open, letting the lake breeze sweep through the space. It gave the place an energy, as if the water itself was watching the progress.

Emily snapped another shot of Liam, his brow furrowed in concentration as he worked a fine chisel along the edge of the hull. Through the viewfinder, she noticed something—an expression that went deeper than focus. It was reverence, a quiet respect for what he was restoring.

"Why this boat?" she asked softly, lowering her camera. "Why the Lady of the Lake?"

Liam paused, his hand resting on the curve of the hull. The silence stretched for a moment, as if he was considering how much to say.

"She reminds me of the lake itself," he said finally. "This boat... she's a piece of history, of everything that came before us. She carried people across these waters—families, supplies, maybe even secrets. Restoring her, it feels like I'm giving something back."

Emily tilted her head. "To the lake?"

"To the lake, to the past... maybe even to myself," Liam admitted, his voice quieter now. "When I was working in the city, I got so disconnected. From this place, from anything real. But here—working with my hands, bringing this back to life—it feels right. Like I'm making peace with something I didn't even realize I'd lost."

Emily felt her chest tighten at his words. She understood that feeling—the need to reconnect, to rediscover something real. She raised her camera again, framing Liam and the boat together, the soft light wrapping around them. It was more than just an image—it was a moment, one that held weight and meaning.

"Do you ever wonder who she carried?" Emily asked, snapping the photo. "Who sat in her, what they talked about, where they were going?"

"All the time," Liam said, his fingers brushing over the wood as if listening for answers. "It's like the lake holds onto those stories, even if we can't see them. Maybe that's why I can't stop working on her—I'm hoping to uncover some of them."

Emily smiled faintly, stepping back to capture a wider shot of the boathouse, the Lady of the Lake framed against the open doors and the shimmering water beyond. "I think you're doing more than restoring her. You're giving those stories a chance to be remembered."

Liam looked up at her then, his expression unreadable but soft around the edges. "And what about you? You've been here just as much as I have, capturing all of this. What are you hoping to uncover?"

Emily hesitated, the question catching her off guard. She thought of the letters tucked carefully back in her cabin, of Ethan's vineyard and its quiet legacy, and of the photos she had taken of Liam's steady, careful work. "The truth, I guess. Every time I look through my lens, I'm looking for something real—something that people can feel when they see it. Whether it's Ethan's wine, Henry's stories, or this boat... there's a connection here. I want people to see that."

Liam held her gaze for a moment, as if trying to read her thoughts. Then, with a slight nod, he turned back to his work, the chisel meeting the wood once more.

Emily stayed a while longer, moving quietly around the boathouse, letting her camera tell the story she couldn't quite put into words. Through her lens, the Lady of the Lake was no longer just a boat—she was a symbol of the valley's mysteries, its history, and the resilience of those who carried its stories forward.

By the time she packed up and stepped outside, the lake was a mirror of the sky, the colors of late afternoon beginning to settle into deep blues and golds. Emily looked back at the boathouse, the light spilling through its open doors. For all the tension and change the valley faced, there was something constant in places like this—in the hands of people like Liam, who worked to preserve what mattered.

As she drove back to the cabin, Emily couldn't stop thinking about what Liam had said—how the lake held onto its stories. She was beginning to believe it, too. And with every photo she took, she felt herself uncovering them, one frame at a time.

Chapter 22

The boathouse smelled of fresh sawdust and varnish, the rhythmic scrape of Liam's sanding filling the air as Emily reviewed her latest photos by the open doors. The late afternoon sun painted the lake in soft golds, and a gentle breeze stirred the edges of the tarp covering the another boat waiting for Liam's talents.

It was the kind of day that made everything feel timeless, a perfect setting for the arrival of Henry. He shuffled in unannounced, his cane tapping lightly against the floorboards.

"Got room for an old man?" he asked, a grin spreading across his weathered face.

"Always," Liam said, gesturing toward a folding chair. "What brings you here today?"

Henry eased into the chair, leaning his cane against the wall. "Thought I'd check on this beauty you're working on," he said, nodding toward the Lady of the Lake. "And maybe share a story or two. You seem to like those, Emily."

Emily glanced up from her camera, her curiosity piqued. "Always. What's the story today?"

Henry leaned back, his gaze drifting toward the lake. "Well, let me tell you about the days before that big ol' bridge came along. Back then, we had boats—real ones—taking people across the lake. The Pendozi and the Sicamous were the lifelines of this valley. If you wanted to get anywhere, you boarded one of those beauties."

Liam paused in his sanding, giving Henry his full attention. "You're talking about the lake steamers?"

"That's right," Henry said, his voice carrying the weight of nostalgia. "*The MV Pendozi and the SS Sicamous*—they were more than just boats. They were the heart of this place, connecting folks from one side of the lake to the other. Remember, there was no bridge back then. You either took the ferry or waited for the steamer."

Emily leaned forward, already envisioning the story through her lens. "What was it like?"

Henry's eyes twinkled. "Oh, it was something. The Sicamous was a grand lady—

ornate, comfortable, a real piece of craftsmanship. People dressed up to ride her, even if it was just a short trip. The Pendozi wasn't as fancy, but she got the job done. Both boats carried passengers, goods, mail—you name it. They kept this valley alive."

He paused, his expression turning wistful. "But you want to hear something really special? Let me tell you about the winter the lake froze over."

"The lake froze over?" Emily repeated, her voice filled with disbelief.

Henry nodded. "Oh, yes. I was just a boy then. The steamboats couldn't run, of course, and folks had to make do. That's when my mother decided she wasn't going to let a little ice stop her. She had four of us in toe—me and my siblings—and we needed to meet the bus to take us to Vancouver."

He chuckled, shaking his head. "So, what does she do? She loads us onto a toboggan, ties us up good and snug, and starts pulling us across the frozen lake. From Kelowna to the Westside. Can you imagine? A mother, out there in the middle of that icy expanse, dragging her kids behind her."

Emily's jaw dropped. "That's... incredible. Weren't you scared?"

"I was too young to be scared," Henry said with a grin. "I thought it was an adventure. My older siblings, though—they knew better. They kept watching the cracks in the ice, holding their breath every time we heard it groan."

Liam leaned against the workbench, clearly captivated. "How far was it?"

"Felt like miles," Henry said. "It was only a mile, but it might as well have been the moon. She made it, though—pulled us all the way across, with suitcases stacked higher than we were tall. That's the kind of woman she was. Strong, determined, and not afraid of a challenge."

Emily lifted her camera, capturing the light in Henry's eyes as he spoke. "What happened to the boats when the first floating bridge was built?"

Henry sighed, his gaze lowering. "They faded into memory, like so much else. The Sicamous—she's up in Penticton now, preserved as a museum. The Pendozi didn't make it, though. Times changed, and the valley changed with them. But I'll tell you this—those boats, and the people who relied on them, they were the heartbeat of the Okanagan."

The room fell quiet as Henry's words settled over them, the soft lapping of the lake filling the silence.

"You ever think about how much history this lake holds?" Liam asked, his voice thoughtful.

"All the time," Henry replied. "It's not just water out there. It's stories. It's lives. And it's people like you two who'll keep those stories alive."

Emily glanced at Liam, a flicker of understanding passing between them. She raised her camera again, capturing the three of them together—the craftsman, the storyteller, and the photographer—connected by the lake and its enduring mysteries.

As the sun dipped lower on the horizon, Henry rose from his chair, his movements slow but deliberate. "Well, that's enough reminiscing for one day. You keep at it, Liam. And Emily—you tell those stories. Don't let them fade away."

"I won't," Emily promised, her voice steady.

Henry tipped his hat, a mischievous glint in his eye, and shuffled out the door.

Liam turned to Emily, a faint smile tugging at his lips. "You're building quite the collection, aren't you?"

Emily nodded, her hand resting lightly on her camera. "I think this valley's stories are building me."

Chapter 23

The golden hues of early evening bathed the valley as Emily and Liam drove along the winding road to Summerhill Pyramid Winery. She'd been looking forward to the dinner Ethan had arranged—a rare moment to step away from work and immerse herself in the company of her new friends. The promise of good food, wine, and conversation was a welcome reprieve from the intensity of the stories she'd been uncovering.

When they arrived, the vineyard sprawled before them, rows of grapevines stretching toward the horizon. The pyramid stood at the winery's entrance, its distinct pyramid structure gleaming in the fading light. The place had an energy to it—both welcoming and mysterious. Emily had heard whispers about the pyramid being aligned with sacred geometry, and now, standing before it, she felt a quiet reverence.

Ethan greeted them at the restaurant entrance, a glass of wine already in hand and a wide grin on his face.

"Welcome to one of the best-kept secrets in the valley," he said, gesturing toward the restaurant. "Nature's Table serves food you'll be dreaming about for weeks."

Liam smirked. "I'm only here because you promised me steak."

"Of course you are," Ethan shot back, his tone playful. "But wait until you taste the wine."

Inside, the restaurant was warm and inviting, with large windows that framed breathtaking views of the vineyard and lake beyond. The air was filled with the rich aroma of roasted vegetables, herbs, and grilled meats. They were seated near the window, the last light of day casting a soft glow across their table.

Ethan poured a generous amount of Summerhill's signature Merlot into their glasses, raising his own in a toast. "To stories, old and new, and to the people who make them worth telling."

Emily clinked her glass against his, then Liam's, smiling as she sipped the wine. It was smooth and full-bodied, the kind of drink that carried the essence of the land it came from.

The meal began with a spread of fresh, seasonal dishes: heirloom tomato salad drizzled with balsamic reduction, house-made bread with whipped herb butter, and charcuterie featuring locally cured meats and cheeses. Emily couldn't help but snap a few photos of the beautifully arranged plates before diving in.

"So," Ethan began, leaning back in his chair, "How's the Lady of the Lake coming along?"

Liam set his fork down, his expression thoughtful. "Slow but steady. Emily's been capturing every moment, so if I mess up, it's well-documented."

Emily laughed. "I think you're doing just fine. Besides, the imperfections are what make it real."

"Spoken like a true artist," Ethan said, raising his glass to her.

As the main courses arrived—perfectly grilled steak for Liam, roasted salmon for Emily, and a vegetarian risotto for Ethan—the conversation shifted to lighter topics. They traded stories about their days: Ethan's antics with the winery staff, Liam's stubborn refusal to use power tools unless absolutely necessary, and Emily's failed attempt to get a squirrel to stay still long enough for a photo.

The laughter was easy and genuine, the kind that made the hours slip by unnoticed.

Eventually, the conversation turned back to the valley itself.

"There's something about this place," Emily said, swirling the wine in her glass. "It's like every corner of it has a story waiting to be told."

Ethan nodded, his gaze drifting out the window. "That's why I stayed. It's not just the wine or the business—it's the connection to the land. There's history here that you can feel, even if you don't know it yet."

Liam leaned back in his chair, his hands resting on the table. "It's the lake for me. Always has been. You can stand on its shores and see the past and present all at once."

Emily glanced between the two men, her heart full. She raised her glass once more. "To the Okanagan, then. And to us, for keeping its stories alive."

They clinked their glasses again, the sound of soft harmony in the cozy restaurant.

As the meal wound down, Ethan insisted on dessert—an indulgent chocolate torte paired with a sweet ice wine that made Emily's taste buds sing. The three of them lingered at the table, the conversation flowing as easily as the wine.

By the time they stepped back outside, the stars were just beginning to emerge, their light reflected on the calm surface of the lake. Emily paused, her camera in hand, and framed a shot of the pyramid glowing softly against the darkening sky.

"This was a good night," Liam said quietly, standing beside her.

"It was," Emily agreed, lowering her camera. "Sometimes, it's nice to just enjoy the moment."

Ethan joined them, his expression content. "We should do this again. Maybe next time, we'll bring Henry—though I'm not sure the winery's ready for him."

Emily laughed, the thought of Henry in this elegant setting both amusing and endearing.

As they parted ways, heading back to their respective corners of the valley, Emily felt a renewed sense of connection—to the land, to the people, and to the stories that had brought them all together.

Chapter 24

The morning sun filtered softly through the cabin windows as Emily sat cross-legged on the floor, surrounded by the now-familiar letters. She had spent hours rereading them, searching for clues—small details that might hint at the people behind the ink. *James and Anna.* Their story lingered like a faint whisper, and Emily felt certain the truth lay somewhere within the walls of this old cabin.

After finishing her coffee, she pulled a dusty wooden box from the corner of the small storage closet. She'd noticed it when she first moved in but had been too focused on her work to look through it. Now, though, every corner of the cabin seemed to call her attention, as if inviting her to uncover what had been left behind.

The box creaked as she lifted the lid. Inside were a few weathered journals, an old map of the Okanagan Valley, and a handful of photographs, their edges curled with age. She carefully picked up the first photo, holding it up to the light. It was a black-and-white image of a modest log cabin nestled by the lake—her cabin. The surrounding land was wild and untamed, a stark contrast to the more developed valley she knew today.

Turning the photo over, she found faint handwriting on the back:
"Cabin near Fintry, 1902. For Anna—my light in this wild place."

Emily's heart skipped a beat. Anna. The same name from the letters. Her hands trembled slightly as she opened one of the journals. The handwriting was familiar— James'.

May 3rd, 1902
The cabin is finally complete, standing quietly by the lake, hidden from the world that refuses to accept us. I built it for her—for us—a place where we could dream of a future untouched by the weight of our families' disapproval. Anna hasn't said much, but I see the doubt in her eyes when she looks at it. She wants to believe in this place, in me, but the world beyond these walls pulls at her. I tell myself that time

will give her hope, that one day she'll see this cabin as our refuge. But deep down, I fear she wonders if a future here can ever truly exist.

Emily sat back, the journal resting in her lap. This was more than a love story—it was a life, a shared dream etched into the very foundations of the cabin. She flipped through the journal, reading entries that detailed James' work as a carpenter and his reflections on the challenges of frontier life. But there were also passages about Anna: her laughter, her strength, and the way she taught him to respect the land.

August 17th, 1902
Anna showed me the cedar grove today, deep in the forest. She says it's sacred, a place her family has visited for generations. I believe her. There's a stillness there that feels almost holy.

The cedar grove. Emily remembered Henry mentioning something about it—a place that tied together the stories of the Syilx people and early settlers.

As she turned the pages, the entries grew more strained, marked with hurried scrawls and darker emotions.

November 12th, 1902
The settlers don't understand. They look at Anna and see difference, not beauty. I hear whispers about us, about her. It's not fair. This valley is big enough for all of us, but they refuse to see it.

The words hit Emily like a punch to the chest. The love James and Anna shared wasn't just a private struggle—it was a challenge to the prejudices of their time. She couldn't help but wonder what had happened next.

She reached the final entry, written with a trembling hand.

December 1st, 1902
Anna didn't come back. I've searched the cedar grove, the lake, the hills—nothing. The snow has begun to fall, and the silence is unbearable. My heart tells me she's out there, but the truth gnaws at me. If she's gone... it's because of this place, because of us.

I'm leaving this journal behind. Maybe one day, someone will find it and remember her the way she deserves.

Tears pricked Emily's eyes as she closed the journal, holding it to her chest. James' words carried the weight of a man who had lost everything—not just his love, but his hope.

She stood, her gaze sweeping the small room, suddenly aware of how much this cabin had witnessed. James had built this place with his hands, hoping for a future that had been ripped away. Anna's laughter had once echoed here, and now, after more than a century, their story was finally resurfacing.

Emily grabbed her camera and headed outside, driven by a new sense of purpose. She captured shots of the cabin in the morning light, the weathered wood, the lake glimmering in the distance, the cedars swaying gently in the breeze. The photos would become part of her Under the Okanagan Sun series—a tribute to lives and love stories that had been lost to time.

Later that day, she found herself back at Liam's boathouse, the journal and photo tucked carefully in her bag. Liam looked up as she entered, his block plane paused mid-stroke.

"Back again?" he asked with a faint smile.

"I found something," Emily said, pulling out the journal and placing it on the workbench. "The cabin—James and Anna. It's all here. He built that cabin for her."

Liam picked up the journal, flipping through the fragile pages with care. "That's... incredible. You're holding history right there."

"I want to find the cedar grove," Emily said softly. "If it's still there, I think it's important. Maybe it's where Anna's story really ends—or begins."

Liam met her gaze, something unspoken passing between them. "I'll go with you."

Emily smiled faintly, feeling that spark of hope again—the one that told her she was exactly where she needed to be.

Chapter 25

The morning mist clung to the hills as Emily and Liam set out along the rugged trail that wound its way through Fintry Provincial Park. Sammy's words about the cedar grove lingered in their minds, guiding their steps as they moved deeper into the forest. Emily's camera swung lightly at her side, ready to capture anything they might find.

The trail was steep in places, the ground uneven from years of wear, but the air carried a freshness that made every breath feel restorative. The towering trees around them grew denser as they climbed, their needles filtering the sunlight into dappled patterns on the forest floor.

"You sure this is the right way?" Liam asked, glancing back at Emily with a raised eyebrow.

Emily smirked, pausing to adjust her footing on a rocky incline. "You're the one who said you've hiked this park before. I'm just trusting your sense of direction."

Liam chuckled. "Fair enough. But if we get lost, it's on you to call for help."

The sound of rushing water grew louder as they ascended, and soon the trail opened to a clearing overlooking Fintry Falls. The cascading water tumbled over the cliffs in a powerful rush, its mist catching the morning light and creating faint rainbows that danced in the air.

Emily stopped, raising her camera to capture the scene. The falls were breathtaking, their sheer energy a stark contrast to the stillness of the forest.

"This is incredible," she murmured, snapping a series of shots.

"Wait until you see what's ahead," Liam said, nodding toward the path that continued to climb alongside the falls.

They followed the trail upward, the sound of the waterfall gradually giving way to the softer rustle of leaves as they moved into a grove of towering trees. The air here was cooler, tinged with the earthy scent of damp wood and moss. The cedars stood like sentinels, their trunks impossibly wide and their branches reaching skyward in a silent testament to their age and resilience.

Emily felt a shiver run through her—not from the cold, but from the sense of history that hung in the grove. It was as if the trees themselves carried the memories of those who had walked here before.

"This must be it," Liam said, his voice low as he stepped into the grove. "The cedar grove Sammy talked about."

Emily moved slowly, her camera raised as she captured the interplay of light and shadow filtering through the canopy above. She felt a profound stillness here, a connection to something ancient and enduring.

"It feels sacred," she said softly, lowering her camera for a moment.

"It is," Liam replied, his gaze sweeping over the grove. "Places like this don't just happen. They're shaped by time, by the land. You can't help but feel it."

As they explored, Emily noticed carvings etched into one of the older trees—symbols that seemed deliberate, though their meaning was lost to her. She snapped a photo of them, hoping to ask Sammy about their significance later.

They found a large, flat stone near the center of the grove and sat down to rest, the sound of the falls a distant murmur behind them.

"Imagine what it must've been like for James and Anna," Emily said, pulling the letters from her bag and spreading them out carefully. "If this was their meeting place, it makes sense. It's hidden, quiet. The kind of place you'd go if you wanted to feel safe."

Liam studied one of the letters, his expression thoughtful. "It's beautiful, but it's not easy to reach. They must've been desperate to have a future together if they came all the way up here."

Emily nodded, her fingers brushing over the worn paper. "Do you think this is where Anna disappeared? The last letter mentioned the cedar grove, but there's no way to know for sure."

Liam was quiet for a moment, then said, "Maybe it's not about where she disappeared. Maybe it's about what this place meant to them. If this was where they came to be together, then it's more than just a grove—it's a piece of their story. And now it's part of ours."

Emily looked up at him, the weight of his words settling over her. She raised her camera again, capturing the way the light danced through the branches, the way the cedars stood steadfast against time.

"I think you're right," she said, her voice steady. "This place isn't about answers. It's about connection. And that's what matters."

They stayed in the grove for a while longer, soaking in the quiet beauty of the moment. As they made their way back down the trail, the sun had climbed higher in the sky, casting the valley in a warm, golden light.

Near the base of the trail, they encountered another hiker, a man with a walking stick and a knowing smile. He nodded toward them as they approached, then gestured back up the trail with his stick.

"You two came that way?" he asked, his tone amused.

Liam nodded, wiping sweat from his brow. "Yeah. It was a climb."

The man chuckled, pointing to a staircase partially obscured by a thicket of trees. "Could've just taken the stairs. They're right over there."

Emily stared at the stairs, then at Liam, before bursting into laughter. "You've hiked this before, huh?"

Liam ran a hand through his hair, his expression sheepish. "I might've forgotten about the stairs."

The man laughed along with them, shaking his head as he continued on his way.

"Well," Emily said, still smiling as they started toward the parking lot, "At least we earned it."

Liam grinned. "Yeah. Let's just keep the stairs between us."

Chapter 26

The light in the boathouse was soft and golden as the afternoon sun filtered through the wide-open doors, glinting off the smooth surface of the Lady of the Lake. Emily sat on a stool nearby, reviewing her latest photos while Liam stood at the workbench, a fresh block of cedar in front of him. His tools were arranged meticulously, and his movements were slow and deliberate as he began sketching lines onto the wood.

"You're starting something new," Emily said, glancing up from her camera.

Liam nodded, his brow furrowed in concentration. "It's a model. Inspired by that love story you uncovered—the one with James and Anna."

Emily straightened, intrigued. "What kind of model?"

"A boat," Liam said, his pencil pausing as he turned the block of wood slightly. "Small, simple. Something that might have carried two people across the lake back then. Something symbolic. I want it to feel like a bridge—not just between the past and present, but between them and us."

Emily felt a flutter of emotion at his words. "That's beautiful. You think their story deserves a bridge?"

Liam looked up, meeting her gaze. "Don't you? They couldn't cross the divide in their time, but maybe we can honor them by acknowledging it—by remembering. And maybe it's more than just their story. It's all the stories tied to this lake, to this valley. They're all connected, aren't they?"

Emily nodded, her heart full as she watched him return to his work. There was something mesmerizing about the way Liam carved the wood, each movement purposeful, as though he was channeling not just his craft but something deeper—something timeless.

Over the next few weeks, Liam worked tirelessly on the boat model, often with Emily nearby, capturing the process through her lens. The cedar took shape under his hands, its graceful curves and fine details revealing a story all their own.

"It's almost like the wood remembers," Liam mused one afternoon as he sanded the hull. "Like it carries the echoes of the past, just waiting for someone to listen."

Emily paused mid-shot, lowering her camera. "That's kind of what I'm doing too, isn't it? Listening to the stories the land has to tell. It's all... under the Okanagan sun."

Liam glanced at her, his expression thoughtful. "That's a good title, you know. For your series."

Emily smiled faintly. "It fits, doesn't it? Everything here—every story, every moment—it's all connected by this place, this light, this sun."

"And it's timeless," Liam added. "The way the sun rises and sets over the lake, just like it always has. It's seen everything—the boats, the bridges, the people. It connects us to the ones who came before."

Emily raised her camera again, capturing the soft glow of the sun on Liam's face as he worked. "You just gave my title more meaning," she said. "Thank you."

When the model was finally finished, Liam invited Emily to the boathouse to see it. It was a small replica, just large enough to fit in his hands, but its craftsmanship was exquisite. The carved cedar gleamed, its shape a blend of traditional Indigenous canoe designs and early settler boats, a tribute to the merging of two worlds.

"It's stunning," Emily said, running her fingers lightly over the smooth surface. "And the carvings? Are those the same symbols we saw in the cedar grove?"

Liam nodded. "I thought it was fitting. A way to tie the boat back to the land, to the people who've always been part of this place."

Liam held the model in the sunlight. Emily lifted her camera, capturing the moment as the light streamed through the boathouse doors. The image was perfect—a symbol of connection, resilience, and the enduring spirit of the Okanagan.

"What are you going to do with it?" she asked.

Liam hesitated, then smiled. "Maybe I'll give it to the museum or to Sammy. Or maybe I'll just keep it here as a reminder that some stories are worth preserving."

Emily nodded, her gaze lingering on the model. "It's more than a bridge, Liam. It's a legacy."

He looked at her, his expression softening. "So is what you're doing, Emily. Don't forget that."

The two stood in silence for a moment, the boat resting between them, a tangible symbol of the stories they had uncovered and the ones they were still creating.

Under the Okanagan sun, past and present continued to converge, their lives woven into the rich tapestry of the valley—a place where love, history, and hope endured.

Chapter 27

The soft hum of the boathouse was punctuated by the rhythmic sound of Henry's voice, the kind that made you want to lean in closer, as though his words carried the very weight of the valley's history. Emily and Liam sat across from him, a shared curiosity pulling them deeper into the world of stories Henry seemed to know so well.

The boathouse felt warmer as the afternoon sun slanted through the windows, the golden light softening the edges of the wooden beams. Henry leaned back in his chair, a mug of coffee in hand, his weathered face lit with both nostalgia and a touch of sorrow as he began to speak.

"The Fintry Queen," he said, his voice tinged with both pride and lament, "She was something else in her day. Built in 1948, a sternwheeler that graced the waters of Okanagan Lake like she owned it. Back then, she ferried people and goods all over the valley, connecting communities that would've been hours apart by road."

Emily leaned forward, her camera resting in her lap, her curiosity drawn to the wistfulness in Henry's tone. "And she passed under the old bridge, right?"

Henry nodded, a faint smile breaking through. "That's right. The original Okanagan Lake Bridge had a lift span on the City Park side, so boats like the Fintry Queen could pass through. It was a sight to see. The cars would line up, and folks would step out, chatting while they waited. It wasn't an inconvenience—it was part of the rhythm of life here. Watching her glide through, with that stern wheel kicking up the water, it was... magical."

Liam glanced over from his workbench, wiping his hands on a rag. "Tell Emily what happened to her? Why she isn't still out there?"

Henry sighed, setting his mug down on the table. "Vandalism," he said, his voice heavy. "After years of being a floating restaurant and event space, she was moored in Kelowna for renovations. But some fools got to her, and what they didn't wreck outright, they made nearly impossible to repair. She's been in storage ever since, neglected and broken."

Emily frowned, the weight of his words sinking in. "That's heartbreaking. To have so much history tied to her, and now she's just... forgotten?"

Henry shook his head. "Not forgotten," he said firmly. "Not by those who remember what she meant. She was more than just a boat—she was a part of this valley, a part of people's lives. And the old bridge? That was part of the story too. The way it lifted to let her through—it was like the land and the water were working together, in harmony."

Emily raised her camera, capturing the sadness and pride in Henry's expression. "And now?" she asked softly. "Do you think there's any hope for her?"

Henry looked out at the lake, his gaze distant. "I'd like to think so. Boats like the Fintry Queen, they're more than just wood and steel. They carry stories, memories. And as long as someone's willing to tell those stories, she's not entirely gone."

Liam crossed his arms, his voice thoughtful. "Kind of like what we're doing here. Bringing something back—not just for us, but for everyone."

Henry grinned faintly. "Exactly. It's not about undoing what's been lost. It's about holding onto what's left and making sure it's not forgotten."

Emily let her camera hang at her side, her gaze drifting to the shimmering surface of the lake. She could almost picture the Fintry Queen in her prime, cutting through the water with quiet dignity, the bridge lifting to honor her passage.

"We'll tell her story," Emily said finally, her voice resolute. "We'll make sure people know what she meant to this place."

Henry tipped his hat in gratitude. "That's all anyone can ask for."

As the light began to fade and the lake turned a deeper shade of blue, the three of them sat in reflective silence, the legacy of the Fintry Queen and the valley's history anchoring them to the moment.

Chapter 28

The community center buzzed with restless energy as locals gathered to discuss the controversial lakefront development proposals. Rows of folding chairs filled quickly, the room charged with a mix of curiosity, frustration, and determination. On one side of the room sat business owners and developers eager to expand tourism, on the other, residents who feared the project would forever alter the delicate balance of life along the lake.

Emily walked in with Liam, her camera slung over her shoulder. She glanced around, spotting Ethan near the front, talking animatedly with a small group of vineyard owners. Henry sat in the back, leaning on his cane, his sharp eyes scanning the room.

"Quite the turnout," Liam murmured.

Emily nodded, already framing her first shot. The tension in the air was palpable, and she wanted to capture it—the faces, the body language, the passion. This meeting wasn't just about tourism or the lake; it was about the identity of the Okanagan Valley itself.

A council member stepped to the podium, tapping the microphone to quiet the room. "Thank you all for coming. Tonight, we'll hear from both sides regarding the proposed marina expansion and waterfront redevelopment. Our goal is to find a solution that benefits the community while respecting the lake's heritage and environment."

The first speaker, a local developer, approached the podium with a confident stride. His presentation was polished, complete with slides showcasing sleek renderings of luxury marinas and waterfront resorts.

"This project represents an incredible opportunity for the valley," he began. "It will bring jobs, boost tourism, and create a world-class destination that showcases the beauty of Okanagan Lake. We're not just building for today—we're building for the future."

A murmur of mixed reactions rippled through the crowd. Some nodded in agreement, while others folded their arms, their expressions skeptical.

Henry leaned toward Emily and whispered, "Future, my foot. He's talking about money, not legacy."

When the developer finished, a local environmentalist took the podium. She spoke passionately about the lake's fragile ecosystem, emphasizing the long-term impact of overdevelopment.

"Okanagan Lake isn't just a resource," she said. "It's a lifeline for wildlife, for families, for traditions that go back generations. If we turn it into a playground for the wealthy, we lose what makes it special. Once that balance is gone, it's gone forever."

Applause erupted from one side of the room while the other remained silent, their tension thick in the air.

Ethan stood next, his calm but firm demeanor commanding attention. "I run a vineyard just up the hill from the lake," he began. "Our business depends on the health of this land, this water, and this community. I'm not against growth—I'm against thoughtless growth. If we expand without considering the lake's needs, we'll destroy the very thing that draws people here."

His words struck a chord, earning nods and murmurs of agreement from both sides of the aisle. But before anyone could speak, Henry cleared his throat and stood, leaning heavily on his cane.

"All due respect to the fancy presentations," he said, his voice rough but steady, "But I've lived here long enough to know that some things don't come back once you lose them. I've seen this lake freeze over in the winter and carry steamboats in the summer. I've seen families rely on it to survive. It's not just a lake—it's a piece of who we are. If you pave over that for a few extra dollars, you're selling out more than land. You're selling out your soul."

The room fell silent, Henry's words hanging in the air like a challenge. Even the developers seemed momentarily disarmed by his candor.

Emily raised her camera, snapping a shot of Henry standing tall despite his frailty, his presence commanding the room. She knew that this moment—this raw, unfiltered truth— was the heart of her project.

The meeting ended without a clear resolution, the debate continuing as people spilled out into the night. Outside, the cool lake breeze carried the echoes of passionate voices, unresolved but determined.

"Think they'll come to an agreement?" Emily asked as she walked with Liam and Ethan toward the parking lot.

"They'll have to," Ethan said. "The question is whether it'll be the right one."

Henry joined them, his cane tapping softly on the gravel. "You can bet they'll keep arguing," he said with a grin. "But that's the beauty of this place—people care enough to fight for it. That's how you know it's worth saving."

Chapter 29

The late afternoon sun cast long shadows across the boathouse as Liam worked with quiet focus, carefully shaping a cedar plank to fit the curve of the *Lady of the Lake's* hull. The ribs, now repaired and sturdy, waited like a skeleton for the skin that would bring the boat to life. Each stroke of his plane shaved off delicate curls of wood, leaving behind smooth, precise edges that would join seamlessly with the others. The scent of fresh cedar filled the boathouse, grounding him in the rhythm of the work.

The rhythmic motion filled the space with a soothing hum, but Liam's thoughts were far from settled. Emily was perched nearby on an overturned crate, reviewing her latest batch of photos. She'd been coming here more often, and though her presence had become something of a comfort, it also unsettled him in ways he couldn't quite name.

"You're unusually quiet today," Emily said, breaking the silence. She glanced up, her eyes catching his as she tilted her head curiously.

"Just thinking," Liam replied, not looking at her. His hands kept moving, though the wood no longer needed sanding.

Emily set her camera aside and stood, brushing her hands on her jeans. She moved closer, leaning against the workbench. "About what?"

He hesitated, then shrugged. "Life. The lake. Everything."

Emily's lips curved into a soft smile. "That's vague."

Liam exhaled, setting the sandpaper down. "I don't know how you do it," he said, finally meeting her gaze. "Just jump into something new, start fresh, like it's easy."

She blinked, surprised by the vulnerability in his voice. "It's not easy. Trust me. Starting over is terrifying, especially when it feels like the whole world is watching you fail."

He leaned against the workbench, crossing his arms. "Then why do it?"

Emily glanced at the open doors, the lake shimmering beyond. "Because staying still feels worse. I needed to come back here, to this place, to figure out what I'd lost. And maybe to figure out what I want."

Her words hung in the air, and Liam felt their weight pressing against his own unspoken fears. He'd built his life around this lake, this boathouse, but what had it cost him? What had he left behind to create this refuge?

"You make it sound so simple," he said softly.

"It's not," Emily replied, her voice equally quiet. "But maybe that's the point. The things that matter most are never simple."

Liam studied her for a moment, the way her hair caught the light, the way her expression shifted between confidence and doubt. He admired her resilience, her ability to find beauty in broken things. But he couldn't shake the fear that letting her in might break something inside him that he'd worked too hard to protect.

"I'm not good at this," he admitted, surprising even himself with the confession.

Emily tilted her head. "At what?"

"Letting people in," he said. "After what happened in the city... I came back here to get away from all of it. The expectations, the pressure, the failures."

Emily's expression softened. "You're not the only one carrying that weight, Liam."

He looked at her, and for a moment, the guarded walls he'd built around himself seemed to falter. "You're different," he said quietly. "I didn't expect someone like you to show up here. And now..." He trailed off, shaking his head as if trying to clear the thought.

"And now what?" Emily asked, her voice barely above a whisper.

Liam hesitated, his eyes searching hers. "Now I don't know what to do with it—with us."

The words hung between them, raw and unpolished. Emily felt her heart tighten, her own fears rising to meet his. She thought of the letters, of James and Anna, and the risks they had taken for love. Could she do the same? Did she even know how?

"Maybe we don't have to figure it out right now," she said finally, stepping closer. "Maybe we just... take it one step at a time."

Liam's eyes softened, and for a moment, the tension in the room seemed to dissolve. He reached out hesitantly, his fingers brushing against hers. It was a small gesture, but it felt monumental—a bridge between the uncertainty of their pasts and the fragile possibility of their future.

Emily didn't pull away. Instead, she met his touch with her own, grounding him in the moment. "We've both been through a lot," she said softly. "But maybe... maybe this place isn't just about the past. Maybe it's about what we can build now."

Liam nodded slowly, his thumb grazing the back of her hand. "Under the Okanagan sun," he murmured, a faint smile tugging at his lips. "Maybe there's room for something new."

Emily smiled back, her heart lighter than it had been in a long time. "I think there is."

The sound of the lake lapping gently against the shore filled the space as they stood together, neither rushing to break the fragile peace they had found. For now, it was enough to know they weren't alone in their uncertainties, that they had found something worth holding onto—no matter how uncertain the road ahead might be.

Chapter 30

The Kelowna Art Gallery was a blend of modern design and artistic warmth, its sleek glass facade reflecting the sunlit sky. Emily stepped through the doors, feeling a mix of excitement and trepidation. The lobby buzzed softly with quiet conversations, the atmosphere one of quiet reverence for art and creativity.

Inside, the walls were alive with work by local and regional artists—paintings, sculptures, and photographs that told the story of the Okanagan through light, texture, and emotion. Emily paused to take it all in, running her hand nervously along the strap of her camera bag.

"Emily!" Susan, the gallery curator, appeared from a side hallway, her tailored blazer and easy smile immediately putting Emily at ease. "I'm so glad you could come. Ethan's told me so much about your work."

Susan led her through the exhibition spaces, their footsteps echoing faintly in the airy, light-filled galleries. Each room was arranged to flow seamlessly into the next, the art carefully curated to showcase the diversity of the valley—its land, its people, its stories.

When they reached a smaller, more intimate space lined with pristine white walls and soft track lighting, Susan turned to her. "This room could be yours, Emily. Your photographs. Your stories. A visual celebration of the Okanagan, both past and present."

Emily blinked, the weight of Susan's words settling over her. "You want me to exhibit my photos here?"

"Yes," Susan said warmly. "We're hosting a special exhibit next month—'Echoes of the Valley'—focused on celebrating the Okanagan's culture, history, and evolution. Ethan showed me a few of your shots, and they're exactly what we're looking for. Your series Under the Okanagan Sun captures something timeless about this place. I'd like you to be the featured photographer."

Emily stared at the blank walls around her, imagining her work hanging there for people to see. The idea felt both thrilling and overwhelming. "I don't know... I'm just getting back into my work. I'm not sure I'm ready for something like this."

Susan smiled gently. "Emily, your photos don't just capture scenes—they tell stories. And this valley needs those stories to be shared. I know it's a big step, but sometimes the best things come when we push ourselves a little further."

Emily looked down, her thoughts spinning. For so long, she'd questioned her abilities, afraid that her failures in Calgary defined her. But now, standing in a gallery full of other artists' work, she realized her photos did matter. They carried pieces of history, moments of beauty, and glimpses of truth— truths the valley itself seemed to whisper under its golden sun.

"I'll think about it," she said quietly, though part of her already knew the answer.

Susan gave her a knowing smile. "Take your time. But don't let doubt stop you, Emily. Your work deserves to be seen."

Chapter 31

The boathouse was quiet, save for the rhythmic creak of the old wooden floorboards as Liam sorted through boxes in the loft. Dust motes swirled in the beams of sunlight filtering through the high windows. Emily sat cross-legged on the floor below, flipping through her camera's photos as she occasionally glanced up, amused by the occasional thud of Liam dropping something heavy.

"What exactly are you looking for up there?" she called, her voice echoing faintly.

"A story," Liam replied, his tone distracted. "Or maybe just proof."

Emily chuckled softly. "You sound like me."

Moments later, Liam's footsteps descended the ladder, and he reappeared, holding an old wooden toolbox under one arm and a crumbling stack of yellowed papers in the other. His expression was a mix of curiosity and reverence.

"This belonged to my grandfather," Liam said, setting the items carefully on the workbench. "I didn't know him well, but my dad always said he spent more time with his tools than his family. Built boats—small ones, like canoes—before he died."

Emily's gaze softened as she looked at the papers he spread out before them. Among them were faded sketches of boat designs, each one marked with handwritten notes in a script that spoke of care and precision.

"These are beautiful," Emily murmured, trailing her fingers over the delicate drawings. "But look at this..."

One of the designs stood out from the others: a hand-carved canoe, its sides etched with symbols Emily recognized. "This looks like what we saw in the cedar grove. It looks like the model you carved."

Liam's brows furrowed as he leaned closer. "It does. But why would he have these markings?"

Carefully, he unfolded a brittle sheet of paper tucked beneath the sketches. It was a faded letter, the ink smudged in places but still legible. Liam began to read aloud.

May 10, 1954
To Mr. Fraser,
I thank you for the canoe you built for my family. You honored our traditions with your work, and my grandfather said it was the finest he'd seen in many years. It is a gift to know there are those who respect our ways and our waters. Should you ever need the lake's guidance, it will be there for you.
—Samuel N'kwala

Liam's voice faltered as he reached the end, his expression unreadable. He ran a hand through his hair, staring at the letter as though seeing it for the first time.

"Samuel N'kwala," Emily repeated quietly. "That's a Syilx name, isn't it?"

Liam nodded slowly, his gaze fixed on the letter. "My grandfather never talked about this. He always said his boats were just work—something he did to get by. I never knew he built canoes for Indigenous families. And he never told me about this connection to the lake."

Emily watched him carefully, understanding the weight of what he was feeling. "Maybe he didn't know how to talk about it. Or maybe he wanted to protect it."

Liam was quiet for a moment, his fingers tracing the edge of the paper. "All this time, I thought I was building boats to find my own way back—to feel connected to this place. But maybe it's been there all along, through him. Through the work he did."

"It's legacy," Emily said softly. "His work, your work—it's part of the same story. And the lake ties it all together."

Liam looked at her then, his expression softer, more open. "It's strange, isn't it? How the past has a way of finding you when you're not even looking for it."

Emily nodded, understanding that truth more than ever. "Maybe the past doesn't disappear—it just waits for someone to pay attention."

Later that afternoon, Liam stood at the boathouse doors, staring out at the lake as the sun reflected in waves of gold and blue. Emily joined him, the soft crunch of her footsteps on the gravel breaking the stillness.

"What are you going to do with all of this?" she asked, nodding toward the sketches and letter resting on the workbench behind them.

Liam exhaled slowly, his hands resting in his pockets. "I think I'll finish what he started. I'll restore one of these canoes, using his designs and the techniques he left behind. Maybe it'll honor what he built—and what this place still means."

Emily smiled, lifting her camera and framing him against the shimmering water. "It's like the lake itself is watching you," she said quietly. "Waiting to see what you'll do next."

Liam turned to her, a faint smile tugging at his lips. "Then I guess I better not disappoint it."

The camera clicked softly, freezing the moment in time—the craftsman and the lake, two pieces of the same story. For Emily, it was another piece of the puzzle, a legacy carried through generations, waiting for someone to uncover it.

And as the sun dipped lower in the sky, casting a warm glow over the valley, Emily felt it again—that unshakable truth that everything here was connected.

Chapter 32

Emily stood at the edge of Evergreen Estates Winery, her camera steady as she framed the final shot. The vineyard spread out before her, rows of grapevines in golden autumn hues, their leaves rustling gently in the breeze. Workers moved rhythmically through the fields, their baskets heavy with ripe fruit, and Ethan Montgomery stood among them, laughing and calling out directions.

"Smile, Ethan!" Emily called teasingly.

Ethan turned with a broad grin, the sun catching the edge of his rugged features. "You're lucky I don't charge you for these photos, Carter!"

She lowered her camera, grinning back. "It's the other way around."

Ethan walked toward her, wiping his hands on his jeans. His shirt sleeves were rolled to the elbows, and his shoulders carried the easy confidence of someone who belonged to the land he worked.

"So, are you happy with the shots?" he asked, gesturing to her camera.

"More than happy," Emily replied. She flipped through the photos on the screen, turning it toward him. "See? I think this one's my favorite."

Ethan leaned closer, inspecting the image. It was a candid shot of him and the crew, baskets of grapes around them, the sunlight catching the vines and their laughter. The warmth of the moment was palpable, a celebration of work, land, and connection.

"That's Evergreen," he said softly, a note of pride in his voice. "You really captured it."

Emily lowered the camera. "It's not just the place. It's you, Ethan. The way you talk about your vineyard, your family—it's clear how much this place means to you."

Ethan's expression softened, his gaze shifting toward the vines. "It's everything to me. My grandfather started this vineyard after the war with nothing but a few cuttings and a lot of grit. My parents built on that, and now it's my turn. I want to keep that alive, not just for my family but for this valley. That's what you're helping me share."

Emily felt a flicker of pride at his words. "I'm glad. I've finished the full set of shots—you've got everything you need for the website and next season's promotions. But... I'd like to include some of these in my exhibit, if you don't mind."

Ethan looked at her, surprise lighting his face. "The gallery show? Really?"

"Why not?" Emily shrugged, her voice thoughtful. "This vineyard is part of the valley's story. It deserves to be seen."

Ethan nodded, his smile widening. "Then, by all means, use them. It's an honor, honestly."

As the wind swept across the vines, carrying the faint scent of grapes and earth, Ethan's gaze shifted to Emily. "You know, I wasn't sure about you when you first showed up. I thought you were another big-city photographer here to tell us what we already knew."

"And now?" Emily teased.

"Now?" Ethan smirked. "I think you're part of this place, whether you realize it or not."

The words settled over her like the sunlight warming the vineyard. Part of this place. She hadn't thought about it that way, but as she stood there, the land stretching endlessly around her, she realized Ethan was right. The Okanagan had started to feel like more than just a setting for her photos. It had become a part of her.

"Well," she said with a small smile, "If you need more photos in the future, you know where to find me."

Ethan laughed softly. "Don't say that unless you mean it, Carter. I'll have you back here for every harvest."

"Deal," she replied with mock seriousness, though deep down, she knew she would return without hesitation.

Later, as Emily loaded her equipment into her car, she paused to take in the scene one last time. Ethan stood at the edge of the vineyard, talking with one of his workers, the sun setting behind the hills in a wash of gold and orange. The light painted everything in rich tones, the kind only the Okanagan could offer.

She raised her camera and snapped the final shot. It wasn't staged or perfect, but it didn't need to be. It was real—Ethan, the vines, and the legacy that connected them all.

As she drove back toward her cabin, the winding road offering glimpses of the lake below, Emily felt a quiet sense of accomplishment. She'd come here for a fresh start, and now, with Ethan's project complete and her exhibit approaching, she could feel it—her purpose coming back to life, as steady and sure as the valley's rhythms.

Chapter 33

The boathouse was bathed in twilight, the sky outside awash in shades of lavender and gold. Emily sat on a worn wooden bench near the open doors, her legs tucked beneath her as she scrolled through the photos she'd taken that day. Liam stood at the workbench, wiping his hands clean of the varnish he'd just applied to the Lady of the Lake. The boat gleamed in the fading light, its restoration nearing completion.

"You're quiet tonight," Liam said, his voice breaking the gentle hum of the lake's evening waves.

Emily looked up, a small smile tugging at her lips. "I'm just thinking."

"About?"

She hesitated, then turned her camera screen toward him. "This."

Liam crossed the space, sitting down beside her as he looked at the image on the screen. It was a shot of him from earlier that afternoon—standing beside the boat, tools in hand, sunlight filtering through the doors and catching in his hair. The expression on his face was focused, serene, almost reverent.

"You caught me working," he said, his tone amused but soft.

"I caught you dreaming," Emily corrected, her voice gentle. "It's more than just work to you, isn't it?"

Liam looked at the photo for a long moment, his gaze lingering on the edges of the boat. "Yeah. I guess it is."

Emily tilted her head, watching him closely. "What is this for you, Liam? I mean, the boats, the boathouse... what do you want this to become?"

Liam leaned forward, resting his elbows on his knees, his gaze fixed on the shimmering lake outside. "It's funny. I came back here thinking I was leaving everything behind— escaping the noise, the pressure, the expectations. I just wanted to build boats in peace. But somewhere along the way, I realized I didn't want to just build boats. I wanted to teach people how to build them too. Workshops, apprenticeships—something that connects people to the craft. To the past, but also to themselves.”

Emily listened quietly, her heart-stirring as she heard the passion in his voice. “That's beautiful, Liam. You're preserving something real—something that people can touch and learn from.”

He turned to her, his expression uncertain. “It's a dream, sure, but... sometimes I wonder if it's enough. Or if I'm just hiding out here, avoiding life.”

Emily shook her head. “You're not hiding. You're building something that matters. And you're not doing it alone. People like Henry, the families who remember the lake's stories... they see what you're doing. You're bringing something back to life.”

Liam was silent for a moment before his gaze met hers. “What about you? You've been capturing everything—me, Ethan's vineyard, the falls, the cedar grove. What do you want all of this to become?”

Emily's fingers brushed over her camera as she thought about the question. “I think I want my work to matter again. Back in Calgary, I lost that. I took photos because I was supposed to, not because I felt anything. But here... everything feels different. The light, the people, the history—it's like I can hear the stories when I look through the lens. My exhibit at the gallery... it's just the start. I want to keep telling these stories. The ones that get lost if no one pays attention."

Liam smiled faintly. "Under the Okanagan sun."

Emily looked at him, surprised. "Yeah. Exactly."

Liam turned toward the lake, his voice quieter now. "You ever think about what comes next? After this—after the boathouse, the photos, the gallery?"

The question hung in the air, heavier than either of them expected. Emily looked out at the lake, the last sliver of sun slipping behind the mountains. "I don't know," she admitted softly. "For a long time, I didn't want to think about it. I was so afraid of failing again. But now... I think I'm starting to believe that whatever comes next might be okay. As long as I'm doing something that matters."

Liam nodded slowly, his gaze distant. "Maybe that's all any of us can hope for."

Emily turned back to him, her voice steady. "You're not failing, Liam. You're building something. And whatever you do next, it'll matter because it's you doing it."

Liam looked at her then, the intensity of his gaze catching her off guard. "Same goes for you, Emily. Your work—you—it's already enough. Don't let anyone, not even yourself, tell you otherwise."

The air between them shifted, the silence rich with unspoken words. Emily's breath caught in her chest, her heart thudding softly against her ribs. For a moment, it felt as though the boathouse, the lake, and the entire valley had grown still, holding its breath with them.

"I think we're both figuring it out," Emily said finally, her voice barely above a whisper.

Liam gave a small, crooked smile, as though acknowledging the space they both hovered in—between the past and the future, between dreams and uncertainties.

Outside, the lake shimmered under the first hints of moonlight, a reflection of possibility. For Emily, it felt like the world was opening up, quietly encouraging her to take the next step, whatever it might be.

And as they sat side by side in the warm glow of the boathouse, neither one moved to fill the silence. Some dreams, after all, didn't need to be spoken to be shared.

Chapter 34

The morning was quiet, the lake a glassy mirror reflecting the low clouds drifting over the mountains. Emily followed Liam along a narrow, overgrown path near the water's edge, her boots sinking softly into the damp earth. They had been out exploring since sunrise, driven by a shared curiosity sparked by Liam's grandfather's sketches and the elder's stories.

"Where are we going?" Emily asked, ducking under a low-hanging branch.

"Henry mentioned something about an old canoe site near here," Liam said, his voice calm but intent. "He said it's been forgotten for decades, buried under sand and brush. If it's there, I want to see it."

Emily adjusted her camera bag and quickened her pace to keep up. "And if we don't find anything?"

Liam looked over his shoulder, his lips curling into a faint smile. "Then, at least we'll have taken a good walk."

The trail opened up to a small, sheltered cove where the lake lapped lazily against the shore. The water here was shallow, the waves revealing glimpses of smooth stones beneath. Driftwood lined the beach, tangled in reeds and moss, as though time itself had forgotten this place.

"There's something about this spot," Emily murmured, taking in the quiet stillness. "It feels... untouched."

Liam nodded, scanning the shoreline with a critical eye. "Henry said it won't be easy to find."

They split up, combing through the driftwood and brush, until Liam's voice called out from further down the shore.

"Emily, over here!"

She hurried to where he stood, half-hidden by a tangle of reeds and sand. Kneeling, Liam had begun clearing away a patch of earth, his hands brushing aside layers of moss and debris to reveal the smooth, weathered curve of wood.

Emily's breath caught. "Is that...?"

"It's a canoe," Liam said softly, his voice edged with awe. "Or what's left of one."

Emily dropped to her knees beside him, gently running her fingers along the visible portion of the canoe. The wood was darkened with age but still solid, its lines graceful and unmistakably handcrafted.

Liam sat back on his heels, wiping sweat from his brow. "This has been here a long time. Probably carved from a single cedar log, like the canoes the Syilx used for centuries."

Emily lifted her camera, framing the shot carefully before snapping a few photos. "You think it's one of theirs?"

"I'd bet on it," Liam said, his tone reverent. "It's not a fishing skiff or anything modern. Look at the way it's shaped. This was built for the lake—light, sturdy, and fast."

Emily leaned back, taking it all in—the canoe, the quiet cove, the trees arching protectively overhead. "It's like it's been waiting here, hidden."

Liam looked at her thoughtfully. "Until now."

Later that day, they stood in the elder Sammy N'kwala's yard, the photos of the canoe spread out between them. Sammy, whose weathered face held years of stories, studied the images in silence, his hands trembling slightly as he touched the edges of the photographs.

"This canoe was built with great care," Sammy said finally, his voice quiet but full of meaning. "These designs—these curves—they belong to my people. The Syilx. Our ancestors used canoes like this to travel, to fish, to trade. The lake was our road, our life."

Liam listened intently, his arms crossed as he leaned against the elder's fence. "Can we restore it?"

Sammy glanced up, his sharp eyes meeting Liam's. "It will take patience, skill, and respect. But yes, it can be done. And it should be done."

Emily felt a thrill of excitement as she looked between the two men. "Could we document it? I mean, the restoration? I'd love to photograph the process—show people how this connects the past and the present."

Sammy's gaze softened as he looked at her. "That would honor it, yes."

Liam nodded, his expression determined. "Then let's do it. I can work on the restoration here, at the boathouse, if you'll guide me through it."

Sammy smiled faintly, the lines in his face deepening. "You have the hands of a craftsman, Liam, and the heart of someone who listens. That's what this canoe needs—care and intention. I'll help you."

By sunset, they were back at the boathouse, unloading tools and supplies Liam had gathered for the canoe's first inspection. The promise of restoration hung in the air, and Emily felt its pull—the chance to preserve something timeless, to tell another story that might otherwise fade.

Liam stood at the edge of the boathouse doors, watching the lake as the sun dipped behind the hills, its light spilling across the water like liquid gold. "This is bigger than just restoring a canoe," he said quietly. "It's about honoring where it came from. It's about connection."

Emily stepped up beside him, her camera at her side. "That's what it's always been about, hasn't it? Connection."

Liam looked at her, his eyes warm. "You're a big part of that, Emily. You're helping people see what's worth holding onto."

She smiled softly, her gaze drifting back to the lake. "So are you, Liam. Maybe that's what we're both doing here—putting things back together."

Chapter 35

The boathouse buzzed with quiet focus as Liam and Sammy worked side by side, the steady rhythm of their tools filling the space. The canoe lay carefully cradled on a pair of sawhorses, its weathered wood cleaned and prepped for restoration. Emily lingered nearby, her camera ready, capturing each step of the process.

Sammy leaned over the canoe, his hands moving with practiced precision as he examined the grain of the wood. "Cedar like this was chosen for its strength and lightness," he said, running his fingers along the curves. "But it's also because of how it speaks to us— it bends and yields when treated right, but it holds steady when it needs to."

Liam watched closely, absorbing the elder's words. "So, it's not just about the wood. It's about understanding it."

Sammy nodded, a faint smile tugging at the corner of his lips. "Exactly. You don't force it. You guide it, shape it, but always listen to what it's telling you."

Emily raised her camera and snapped a photo, the contrast of Sammy's weathered hands against the smooth cedar creating a striking image. "It's like the canoe has its own story," she said softly.

"It does," Sammy replied, glancing at her. "Every piece of it—from the tools used to carve it to the water it touched—holds meaning. That's why we respect it."

Liam reached for a hand plane, hesitating slightly before starting to shave away a thin layer of damaged wood. Sammy placed a hand on his shoulder, stopping him.

"Not like that," Sammy said gently. "Here, let me show you."

He picked up a curved knife—a traditional tool Emily hadn't seen before—and handed it to Liam. "This is called a crooked knife. It was used by my ancestors for shaping wood. Hold it like this," he said, demonstrating, "And pull toward yourself in smooth, controlled strokes. Let the wood tell you how much to take."

Liam mirrored the movement, his hands tentative at first. The knife glided along the canoe's edge, peeling back a delicate ribbon of cedar. He glanced at Sammy, a mix of concentration and satisfaction in his expression.

"You've got it," Sammy said with a nod. "It's about rhythm, not force. Once you find it, the wood will follow."

Emily stepped closer, capturing the moment—the elder teaching the younger, their shared focus on a craft rooted in tradition. She lowered her camera and smiled. "That's incredible. It's like the past and present working together."

Sammy chuckled. "That's exactly what it is. These techniques aren't just for building canoes—they're a way of thinking. Patience. Respect. Care. That's how you honor the work."

As the afternoon light slanted through the boathouse, Sammy moved on to showing Liam how to use steam to soften the cedar for bending. He explained how Syilx canoe builders would use hot stones and water to create the right conditions, adapting the wood without breaking it.

"This way," Sammy said, gesturing to the steaming setup they had improvised, "You let the wood decide how far it can bend. Push too hard, and it'll crack. But if you give it time, it'll surprise you."

Liam worked silently, his brow furrowed in concentration as he shaped the softened wood, bending it gently into place. When he looked up, Sammy was smiling.

"You're learning," Sammy said simply.

By the time the sun dipped low on the horizon, casting the boathouse in golden hues, the canoe was beginning to take shape. The rough edges had been smoothed, and the repairs were already starting to blend with the original craftsmanship.

Emily leaned against the doorframe, her camera hanging at her side, watching the two men work. "This isn't just restoring a canoe," she said softly. "You're preserving something bigger than that."

Sammy turned to her, his voice quiet but firm. "It's not just about what we're building. It's about how we build it. These techniques—they've been passed down for generations. Every time they're used, they carry the spirit of those who came before."

Liam glanced at Sammy, his expression thoughtful. "And now you're passing them on to me."

Sammy's smile deepened. "That's how it works. We carry what we've been given and share it, so it's never lost."

The three of them stood together in the quiet of the boathouse, the canoe resting between them like a bridge connecting past and present. The air was filled with the scent of cedar and steam, the sounds of the lake lapping gently against the shore.

Emily lifted her camera and took one last photo as the light faded, capturing the moment—the elder, the craftsman, and the storyteller, each adding their part to a legacy that would endure.

Chapter 36

The scent of roasted corn, baked apples, and sweet cinnamon drifted through the crisp autumn air as Emily wandered down the gravel path leading into the heart of the fall festival, she took in the breathtaking view of East Kelowna.

The event was perched high on the hill, nestled in a golden orchard where rows of apple and pear trees framed the scene. Their autumn leaves rustled gently in the breeze, adding splashes of amber and red to the vibrant setting. Beyond the orchard, the city and Okanagan Lake shimmered in the distance, the landscape alive with the glow of the season.

The community had turned out in full force. Children ran between hay bales stacked like forts, while families browsed tables laden with local produce, handmade crafts, and steaming mugs of cider. Laughter mingled with the faint sounds of a fiddle playing in the distance, the atmosphere alive with warmth and celebration.

Emily adjusted her camera bag and lifted her lens, snapping a shot of a row of sunlit pumpkins lined up by a wooden stand, their vivid orange hues glowing like lanterns against the grass. *This,* she thought, *was the Okanagan at its finest—simple, beautiful, and full of life.*

She spotted Ethan near a booth offering wine tastings, deep in conversation with a group of vineyard owners. He caught her eye and grinned, lifting a glass as though to toast her. "Carter!" he called out, weaving his way toward her. "Glad you made it!"

"I wouldn't miss it," Emily replied, smiling. "This is incredible. It feels like the whole valley's here."

"That's because they are," Ethan said proudly, his gaze sweeping over the festival. "The harvest's winding down, and this is our way of celebrating. A reminder that we all work hard, but we know how to come together when it matters."

Emily nodded, absorbing the sentiment as she watched people laughing, talking, and sharing food. "It's special," she said softly. "There's a resilience here—a pride."

Ethan's grin softened into something more thoughtful. "That's what I love about this place. No matter how much it changes, that spirit holds on."

"Speaking of spirit," Emily teased, pointing to his glass, "You might want to pace yourself. I hear there's dancing later."

Ethan laughed, raising his hands in surrender. "I'll save you a spot if you're brave enough."

"Pass," Emily replied with a grin. "I'll stick to taking pictures."

Further into the festival, Emily spotted Liam near a blacksmith's stall, deep in conversation with the artisan demonstrating traditional metalwork. He was focused, his hands resting in his pockets as he listened, a small smile tugging at the corners of his mouth.

"Is this where you're hiding?" Emily teased as she approached, earning an amused glance from Liam.

"Not hiding," he replied. "Just appreciating good craftsmanship."

She raised her camera and snapped a quick shot of him beside the glowing forge. "You fit right in."

Liam rolled his eyes but didn't argue. "How's the festival treating you?"

Emily looked around, the sound of music, laughter, and chatter filling the space. "It's... perfect. I feel like I could spend hours here and still not capture it all."

He glanced at her, his expression softer now. "You don't have to capture everything, you know."

Emily lowered her camera. "What do you mean?"

"Sometimes it's okay to just be part of it," Liam said, gesturing to the scene unfolding around them. "The stories, the memories— they don't all have to live behind a lens."

His words caught her off guard, settling somewhere deeper than she expected. She turned to look at the festival with fresh eyes— the families sharing meals, the farmers shaking hands, the children pulling their parents toward the caramel apple stand. For a moment, Emily let herself feel it all without reaching for her camera.

"You're right," she said softly. "It's nice to just... be here."

Liam gave her a small, knowing smile. "Told you."

As the sun dipped lower in the sky, a makeshift stage near the center of the meadow came to life, with a band striking up a lively tune. Couples drifted toward the open area in front, hands clasped as they twirled to the music.

Ethan reappeared at Emily's side, offering her a cup of mulled cider. "I'll ask one more time," he said, grinning mischievously. "Care to dance?"

Emily shook her head, laughing. "Not a chance. But you go. I'll be here—enjoying my cider and watching you embarrass yourself."

Ethan gave a mock bow. "Suit yourself, Carter. You don't know what you're missing."

She watched as he joined the dancers, spinning a laughing woman in a colorful scarf under the string lights. The music swelled, and the crowd cheered as more people joined in, their movements carefree and full of joy.

Emily turned to Liam, who had settled beside her, hands tucked into his coat pockets.

"Are you going to join them?" she asked, smirking.

Liam snorted softly. "Not likely. I'm no Ethan."

She grinned, lifting her cup to her lips. "You're telling me you can build a boat from scratch but can't manage a two-step?"

"Exactly," he replied, deadpan, earning a laugh from her.

As the stars began to prick the darkening sky, the festival quieted, families gathering their children and vendors packing up their booths. The hum of the evening lingered, though, like the memory of something precious.

Emily stood with Liam and Ethan at the edge of the orchard, the three of them taking it all in—the lights, the music still echoing faintly, the way the lake glimmered under the moonlight.

"It's nights like these," Ethan said, his voice low, "That reminds you why we hold onto this place."

Liam nodded, his gaze fixed on the lake. "It's worth holding onto."

Emily said nothing, but her chest swelled with a quiet gratitude. She didn't need her camera to capture this moment. The feeling of connection—to the land, the people, and the stories they shared—was enough.

As her fingers intertwined with Liam's, Emily felt it again—the unshakable pull of this place. Under the Okanagan sun and now beneath its stars, it was alive, resilient, and beautiful in ways that defied explanation. It wasn't something to be described—it was something to be felt.

Chapter 37

*L*ast night had ended so peacefully, the stars casting their soft glow across the lake as they walked back to his truck. The warmth of Liam's hand in hers lingered, a quiet connection that had felt easy—uncomplicated. But somewhere between the stars and the drive back to her cabin, that fragile ease had unraveled, slipping into a silence she couldn't quite place.

This morning, the boathouse was calm in appearance but heavy in feeling. The scent of cedar and varnish hung in the air as it always did, yet there was something else—a stillness thick with everything unspoken.

Emily stood near the open doors, her camera bag hanging loosely at her side, her gaze fixed on Liam. He was at the workbench, his back to her, the motion of his hands slower, more deliberate, as though the act of steadying the wood might steady him too.

"You're quiet this morning," Emily said softly, but the question behind her words hung in the air.

Liam paused, his fingers brushing the edge of the hull he'd been sanding. "Not much to say, I guess."

Emily's brows furrowed as she stepped forward. "You're sure about that?"

For a beat, the boathouse seemed to hold its breath. Outside, the lake lapped gently against the shore, oblivious to the tension settling between them.

Liam exhaled, finally turning to meet her gaze. "I thought last night was... good."

"It was," Emily said quickly, her voice softer now. "But it feels like something shifted, and I don't know why."

Liam paused, the tool stilling in his hands before he set it down with deliberate care. "I don't know what you want me to say, Emily."

"Anything would be a good start." She stepped forward, her boots echoing softly on the wooden floor. "You've barely said two words to me since the festival. Did I do something? Or are we just pretending none of this—us, whatever this is—matters?"

Liam turned slowly, his expression guarded. "It's not that simple."

"Why not?" Emily shot back, her voice rising slightly. "You talk about connection and legacy like it's all you care about, but when it comes to letting someone in—really in—you just shut down."

Liam's jaw tightened, his gaze shifting to the boat he'd been restoring for weeks. "I've let people in before, Emily. I know how it ends."

The words hung in the air, sharp and cutting. Emily stared at him, feeling the sting of his unspoken meaning. "So, what? You're just going to spend your life hiding in this boathouse, convincing yourself that no one else is worth the risk?"

Liam's head snapped up, his voice cool but edged with hurt. "I'm not hiding."

"Then what are you doing?" Emily challenged, her hands falling to her sides. "Because from where I'm standing, it looks like you're afraid to feel anything that you can't control."

Liam's face darkened, his voice low but firm. "You don't know anything about what I've been through, Emily."

"Then tell me!" she pleaded. "You think I don't understand loss? Failure? Do you think I came back here because I had it all figured out?"

Liam turned away, his shoulders stiff, his silence cutting deeper than his words ever could. Emily took a shaky breath, the emotion rising in her chest.

"Liam, I don't need you to have all the answers," she said quietly, her voice breaking slightly. "But I need to know that I'm not the only one trying here. I can't keep guessing where I stand with you."

Liam let out a long breath, his hands bracing against the edge of the workbench as though the weight of her words pressed on him. "It's not that I don't feel anything, Emily. That's the problem—I feel too much. And I don't know if I can carry that again."

The admission hit her like a wave, softening her frustration into something more fragile. "What are you so afraid of?" she whispered.

Liam turned to face her then, his eyes shadowed with memories he hadn't shared. "Of losing something I care about. Of losing you."

Emily's chest tightened as she took a step closer, her voice steady despite the emotion rising in her throat. "You don't get to push me away because you're afraid of what might happen. Life isn't about protecting yourself from pain, Liam. It's about letting people in anyway—even when it's hard."

For a long moment, neither of them spoke. The silence was raw and unflinching, the space between them filled with everything they weren't saying.

Finally, Liam shook his head, his voice rough. "I'm not sure I know how to do that."

Emily swallowed hard, forcing herself to hold his gaze. "Then figure it out. Because I'm not going to stand here and fight for someone who's already decided they're going to lose."

The words landed like a blow, and Liam looked away, his face pale in the fading light. Emily waited, hoping he'd say something—anything—that would tell her he was willing to fight for this, for her. But the silence stretched, and the only sound was the faint lapping of the lake against the shore outside.

She turned slowly, the weight of the moment pressing on her shoulders. "I'll see you around, Liam," she said softly, before walking out of the boathouse.

The door swung shut behind her, and Liam stood alone, the emptiness of the space suddenly overwhelming. He ran a hand through his hair, his breath unsteady as he looked at the boat he'd poured himself into—

a project that, for all its progress, still felt incomplete.

Outside, Emily walked toward her cabin, the cool lake air biting at her cheeks as tears threatened to spill. She wasn't angry anymore. She was just tired—tired of fighting for something Liam couldn't see, or wouldn't allow himself to believe in.

As she turned a corner back to the cabin, she stole one last glance at the boathouse.

It looked the same as ever—solid, sturdy, unshaken—but inside, she knew, it held a man who was anything but.

Chapter 38

The morning light streamed through the cabin's small windows, catching on floating specks of dust as Emily sat cross-legged on the floor, her camera set aside for once. Spread before her was a growing collection of letters, photographs, and fragments of history she'd uncovered over the past few weeks. The story of Anna and James—their forbidden love, the hidden cabin—had become more than an old secret. It was a thread that wove through everything she and Liam had uncovered, and she could feel herself getting closer to understanding its full significance.

A piece of folded parchment caught her eye, tucked at the bottom of the old box she'd found behind a loose board in the wall. Carefully, she unfolded it, revealing a letter written in the same flowing script as James' previous ones.

November 3, 1905
Anna,
The cabin is nearly finished. I've carved your name into the beam above the hearth, where it will stay for as long as the wood holds. I dream of the day we no longer have to hide—that this place can be ours without fear of being found. I spoke to a boatbuilder this week, a young man named Fraser, who has been restoring small canoes near the lake. I told him little, but I've asked him to help me build something— something we can use to cross the lake safely and quickly if we ever need to. He works with care, and though he doesn't know my full reason, he sensed this project mattered. He didn't ask questions.
Soon, we'll have a way out, a way forward. Until then, my love, hold onto hope.
—James

Emily's breath caught as she read the final lines. "Liam's grandfather," she whispered, the realization settling in her chest. The connection had been there all along—James had turned to Fraser to help him, perhaps unknowingly tying his and Anna's story to Liam's family legacy.

She read the letter again, more slowly, this time, her fingers brushing over the paper. The cabin wasn't just a meeting place—it had been a symbol of hope, a dream of freedom for two people who'd been denied it. And the boat, the one Liam's grandfather had built, had been part of that dream.

The faint sound of a car approaching broke her thoughts. Emily tucked the letter carefully into her bag before stepping outside to find Liam pulling up in his truck, its tires crunching on the gravel drive.

"Morning," he said as he climbed out, carrying a thermos in one hand and a small notebook in the other.

"Morning," Emily replied, smiling faintly. "Here to apologize?"

Liam ignored her and held up the notebook. "Henry gave me this yesterday. Said it was my grandfather's old project log. I thought you'd want to see it."

Still upset but interested in his find, Emily gestured for him to come inside, excitement fluttering in her chest as they sat across from each other at the cabin's small kitchen table. Liam opened the notebook, its edges worn and the pages faintly yellowed. Inside were neat entries describing boat restorations, materials used, and names of clients—until one entry stood out.

October 1905, A man came today, asking for something small but fast—something he could use on the lake. Didn't say much about why, but the way he talked, I knew it wasn't just about fishing. Told him I'd help.

Liam exhaled, his thumb tracing the corner of the page. "It's him, isn't it? James."

Emily nodded, pulling the letter she'd found from her bag and sliding it across the table. Liam read it slowly, his brows furrowing.

"He carved her name into the beam above the hearth," Liam murmured, glancing up at Emily. "This cabin—it's part of their story."

Emily looked around, suddenly seeing the small, rustic space through new eyes. "It was a promise—something they were building together."

Liam sat back, his expression thoughtful. "And my grandfather—he helped without even knowing the whole truth. Maybe that's why he never talked about it. He sensed it was bigger than him."

Emily leaned forward, her voice soft. "Don't you see, Liam? Your family's legacy and this cabin—they're connected. The boats, the land, the people—it's all tied together. You're not just restoring wood and nails. You're preserving stories. Stories like James and Anna's."

Liam ran a hand over his face, the weight of the realization settling over him. "I never thought of it like that. I've been so focused on the work itself, I didn't stop to see what it means."

Emily smiled gently. "Sometimes we get so caught up in building that we forget what we're building for."

Liam looked at her then, something unspoken passing between them. "And what about you? You're part of this now, too."

"I think we're both part of it," she replied softly. "It's not just their story. It's the valley's story. And maybe... it's ours, too."

The silence that followed wasn't heavy this time. It was filled with understanding—a sense that the pieces of the past, scattered and forgotten, were finally coming together.

Liam stood and walked to the hearth, running his fingers lightly along the beam above it. "If Anna's name is here, it's faint, but I'll find it."

Emily joined him, raising her camera to take a shot of the cabin's heart—the beam that carried their names, their story, and the legacy of everything this place had meant.

"Do you think she really left him?" Liam asked quietly.

Emily lowered her camera, her voice soft. "I don't think she did willingly."

Liam nodded, the words settling over him like the quiet of the cabin. "I wish I knew the whole story."

Outside, the lake stretched toward the horizon, shimmering under the soft morning sun. For Emily and Liam, in that moment, the weight of everything unsaid didn't feel so heavy anymore.

Chapter 39

The boathouse was alive with the golden glow of late afternoon as Emily stepped inside, the soft hum of activity pulling her into the space. The canoe rested on sawhorses, its restoration nearly complete, the wood gleaming under careful care. Sammy N'kwala stood nearby, his hands tucked into the pockets of his weathered jacket, his sharp eyes studying the canoe with quiet reverence.

Liam placed the auctioned boat model on the workbench beside the canoe. Its polished surface caught the light, the intricate carvings a testament to its craftsmanship. "You said this model meant something," Liam said, his tone curious but measured. "Something connected to the symbols on the canoe and in the grove."

Sammy stepped closer, his fingers tracing the carvings on the model's hull. "These symbols are more than decoration," he began, his voice low and deliberate. "They're messages. Protection. Guidance. They tell stories of the land and the people who travel it. But these," he pointed to a series of flowing designs near the bow, "these are unique. They were used sparingly, meant to mark something sacred—a journey of purpose, of love."

Emily moved closer, her camera hanging at her side. "And the model?" she asked softly. "How does it tie into the canoe we found?"

Sammy let out a long breath, as though reaching into the depths of his memory. "The model was a tribute," he said. "A symbol of something bigger. My grandfather used to tell me about a young man—James. He was from a settler family, and he fell in love with a Syilx woman, Anna. Their love was strong, but their families wouldn't allow it. They built a plan— James came to a boatbuilder, your grandfather, Liam, and together they crafted a canoe to carry him and Anna across the lake. The carvings were added by Anna's brother, symbols to protect their journey."

Liam glanced at the canoe, his expression heavy with thought. "But it didn't happen. The letters we found said that she never showed up."

Sammy's lips pressed into a thin line. "That's what people thought. But my grandfather heard a different ending. He said Anna knew the risk—her family was against the union, and she feared they'd come after them. So she sent a message to James, telling him to meet her at a different time and place. The canoe they built? It was meant to be a decoy, something to distract their families. If they saw it hidden or abandoned, they'd assume the worst and stop looking."

Emily's breath caught. "Do you think it worked? That they actually made it?"

Sammy nodded slowly. "There are whispers—stories passed down. My grandfather always said he believed they found peace somewhere else. Far enough that neither family could interfere. Anna was clever, and James was determined. It took a few years, and James had to play the heartbroken dreamer, but if anyone could have done it, it was them."

Liam's gaze returned to the canoe, his fingers brushing the smooth surface of the hull. "And the model?"

"It was left behind," Sammy said. "A marker, maybe. A reminder of what they'd fought for. My grandfather said it was found years later by someone who didn't understand its meaning. They kept it, polished it, and eventually, it ended up at that auction. But the symbols—it's clear it was meant to tie back to the canoe. The two were part of the same story."

Emily lifted her camera and framed the scene, capturing Sammy's weathered hands resting on the model, the canoe gleaming in the background. "It's incredible," she murmured. "Their story, their love—it's still here, in these pieces."

Sammy's gaze softened as he looked at her. "That's the power of stories. They don't fade if someone remembers to tell them."

Later that evening, Liam and Emily returned to her cabin. A quiet energy seemed to linger between them, shaped by Sammy's words and the history they had uncovered. Liam walked to the hearth, his hand brushing over the beam above it. "There," he said softly, pointing to the faint etchings they had found before.

Emily brought over a lantern, its light spilling across the wood to reveal the familiar carvings—the same flowing designs that adorned the canoe and the model.

"It's here," Emily whispered, her voice filled with awe. "The same symbols. James really did carve them into this place."

Liam nodded, his hand tracing the lines. "He built this cabin for her. For them. It was meant to be their home."

Emily knelt beside him, her fingers brushing the symbols. "They tried to build a life together. Even if no one believed in them, they believed in each other."

For a moment, they sat in silence, the weight of the story filling the small space. It felt as though James and Anna's presence still lingered here—a love so strong it refused to be forgotten.

Liam broke the quiet, his voice thoughtful. "Maybe we don't know the whole story. Maybe they did find peace somewhere else. Maybe the canoe and the letters were their way of throwing everyone off their trail."

Emily smiled faintly, her heart full. "I'd like to think so. That they were willing to risk everything to be together."

Liam's fingers lingered on the carvings, his voice steady. "We're going to finish what they started. Finish restoring the canoe, honor their journey. And maybe, when it's done, we return it to the land and the people it belongs to."

Emily placed a hand lightly on his arm, their shared determination filling the room. "And we'll tell their story. The way it was meant to be told."

Chapter 40

The Kelowna Art Gallery hummed with quiet anticipation as Emily stood near the entrance, taking it all in. The space had been transformed for the evening—her photographs displayed with an elegance that somehow captured both the intimacy and vastness of the valley she had come to love.

Each wall told a story, carefully curated to reflect the beauty, resilience, and interconnectedness of the Okanagan. Quiet murmurs filled the room as visitors leaned closer to study the textures, light, and emotions woven into every frame.

Susan, the gallery curator, approached with a warm smile, a glass of wine in hand. "You did it, Emily. It's stunning."

Emily scanned the room, her chest tightening with pride. "Thank you," she replied softly. "It's more than I imagined."

The first display wall focused on the boats, featuring Emily's photographs of the *Lady of the Lake* restoration and the forgotten Syilx canoe they had uncovered. One frame showed Liam standing by the restored canoe, his hand resting on the intricate carvings along its hull, glowing in the late afternoon light. Another captured Sammy N'kwala tracing the same symbols, his weathered hands imbued with reverence, the lake shimmering behind him like liquid glass.

Beneath the photographs, a small plaque read:

"The Canoe: A vessel of connection and hope. Tied to stories of resilience, love, and history, these boats once carried people across the waters of the Okanagan, honoring the land and those who care for it still."

Liam stood nearby, studying the photos with quiet pride. Emily joined him, her voice soft. "It's beautiful, isn't it? The way it all came together."

He turned to her, his expression sincere. "You didn't just capture the wood or the symbols. You captured what they mean."

Emily's smile was faint but warm. "It's their story, Liam. I just helped tell it."

The next section brought visitors into the heart of the vineyard. Ethan's Evergreen Estates was displayed in vivid tones of gold and green. One photograph showcased endless rows of vines kissed by the early morning sun. Another framed Ethan, his hands dirtied with earth, standing among the harvest crew with baskets of deep purple grapes at their feet.

A third image drew visitors in—a candid shot of Ethan laughing with his workers during the crush, sleeves rolled up and the blur of activity swirling around him. The energy of the moment radiated from the frame, a testament to the life and care that ran through the vineyard.

Beneath the images, Emily had written: "The Vineyard: A testament to legacy and labor. The land gives back to those who care for it, season after season. Each bottle carries a piece of history."

Ethan approached as she lingered there, holding two glasses of wine. "You made us look pretty good," he teased, handing her a glass.

"You did that yourselves," Emily replied with a smile. "I just showed people what's already there."

Ethan's gaze softened. "You've got a gift, Emily. This valley needed someone like you to show it to the world."

She felt the sincerity behind his words and lifted her glass. "To Evergreen."

"To you," Ethan replied warmly.

At the back of the room, the Lady of the Lake became the emotional anchor of the exhibit. A series of breathtaking photographs depicted its transformation. One showed Liam sanding its ribs, the golden light catching the wood's grain as though it had waited decades to shine again. Another captured the finished boat, its sails catching the late afternoon sun, floating gracefully on the lake.

The central image held the room's attention: the Lady of the Lake, her reflection perfectly mirrored on calm water, framed by the Okanagan sky. She wasn't just a boat—she was a symbol of restoration and forward movement, an homage to the past, and a promise for the future.

Beneath the photos, a plaque read: "The Sailboat: A story of renewal and craftsmanship. The past lives within the wood, but the journey forward is in our hands. We build, we restore, we move on—under the Okanagan sun."

Liam lingered near the display, a small crowd gathered around him, murmuring about the care and dedication the sailboat had received. Emily stepped closer, catching his eye.

"You really tied it all together," he said as she reached him.

"Because it is tied together," Emily replied. "The valley, the boats, the vineyard—it's all connected. It's all part of the same story."

Liam nodded, his gaze drifting back to the photos. "And you gave that story life, Emily. You made sure it won't be forgotten."

As the evening wore on and the gallery filled with conversation and quiet admiration, Emily stood back and let it all sink in. The photographs weren't just images—they were fragments of the valley's soul, woven through with history, connection, and love.

Susan joined her again, her smile full of pride. "People are already asking about prints and tours. You've done something special here."

Emily glanced around the room, her heart full. "It's not just my story. It's the valley's. I just gave it a chance to be seen."

Later, stepping outside into the cool autumn air, Emily let the quiet of the evening wrap around her. The stars were beginning to peek through the darkening sky, and the lake shimmered faintly under the moonlight.

Liam joined her, his hands tucked into his pockets. "You're proud of it, aren't you?" he asked softly.

"I am," Emily admitted, her gaze lingering on the horizon. "For the first time in a long time, I feel like I've done something that matters."

Liam stepped closer, his voice low. "You have."

Emily turned to him, her smile gentle. "We both have. Under the Okanagan sun."

Liam nodded, and for a moment, they stood together in companionable silence. The valley's stories—its people, its history, its beauty—had found a new life. And so, it seemed, had they.

Chapter 41

The boathouse was buzzing with energy, a blend of sawdust, tools, and quiet chatter filling the space. The once-solitary haven of Liam's craft had evolved into something far more dynamic—a place alive with learning and collaboration.

It had started at the gallery, where Liam had lingered by the photos of the Lady of the Lake, quietly listening as visitors admired the boat's transformation. That night, over glasses of wine, he told Emily and Ethan about the unexpected interest his work had sparked.

"People kept asking for my card," Liam had said, leaning against the bar with a mix of amusement and disbelief. "A few even asked if I'd teach them how to build or restore boats."

Ethan, holding a glass of wine, had grinned. "And? What'd you say?"

Liam shrugged, but the hint of a smile tugged at the corner of his mouth. "I didn't know what to say at first. But the more I thought about it, the more it made sense. It's time to share this craft—keep it alive, you know?"

Emily's eyes lit up. "You should absolutely do it. Think of the stories you could preserve, the skills you could pass on. It's like bringing the past into the present."

Weeks later, Liam stood in front of a small group in the boathouse, demonstrating how to shape a rib for a traditional wooden sailboat. The class was a mix of curious locals and hobbyists, each with their own reason for being there. Some wanted to learn the craft, the history drew others, and a few just wanted to build something with their own hands.

"Boatbuilding isn't just about the end result," Liam said, his hands steady as he guided the curved knife along the wood. "It's about patience, respect for the materials, and understanding that every piece has a role. You're not forcing the wood—you're working with it."

Emily watched from the edge of the room, her camera capturing the concentration on the faces of the participants, the careful movements of their hands as they mimicked Liam's techniques. She loved seeing him in this element—sharing his knowledge, connecting with people through his craft.

Sammy N'kwala joined them occasionally, bringing his own perspective to the workshops. He shared traditional Syilx methods, blending them seamlessly with Liam's modern techniques.

"Steam is one of the oldest tools we have," Sammy explained during one session, holding up a strip of cedar. "When you use it to soften the wood, you're not just shaping it—you're listening to it. It's a conversation, not a command."

Liam nodded, echoing Sammy's sentiment as he addressed the group. "That's the key to this work. It's not about rushing or controlling—it's about finding the balance between structure and flow."

By the end of the class, the students had finished their first small projects—sections of a canoe's ribbing, carefully shaped and sanded under Liam and Sammy's guidance. The satisfaction on their faces was palpable as they laid their pieces on the workbench, admiring the results of their labor.

Ethan arrived as the session wrapped up, leaning against the doorframe with a grin. "Looks like you've got yourself a full-blown operation here."

Liam chuckled, wiping his hands on a rag. "Didn't think it would take off this quickly, but it's been good. Feels like I'm doing something that matters."

Emily stepped up beside him, her camera hanging at her side. "You are, Liam. You're building more than boats—you're building a legacy."

He glanced at her, his expression softening. "Couldn't have done it without you two. This all started with the stories we uncovered together."

Ethan clapped a hand on Liam's shoulder. "Well, don't forget us when you're famous."

Liam laughed, shaking his head. "Don't hold your breath on that."

As the students trickled out, each thanking Liam and Sammy for the experience, Emily lingered by the lake. Liam joined her, the scent of cedar and varnish still clinging to him.

"Feels good, doesn't it?" Emily said, her voice quiet.

"Yeah," Liam replied, his gaze fixed on the shimmering water. "Feels like I'm finally giving something back."

Emily turned to him, a small smile on her lips. "You're not just giving back. You're showing people what's worth holding onto."

Liam nodded, the weight of her words settling over him. Together, they watched the lake, the reflection of the light fading into the horizon, knowing that the legacy they were building wasn't just about the past—it was about the future, too.

Chapter 42

The boathouse buzzed with activity as Liam adjusted the sawhorses under the newly restored canoe, ensuring it was balanced just right. The rhythmic sound of tools against wood filled the space until Ethan's voice cut through.

"Look who I found wandering around Kelowna," Ethan said, stepping into the boathouse. Claire followed, her warm smile lighting up the room.

Liam straightened, wiping his hands on a rag. "Claire Bennett," he said, a small grin tugging at his lips. "I was wondering when you'd show up again."

Claire laughed lightly, extending her hand. "Good to see you again, Liam. I hear you've been busy. This canoe project has everyone in town talking."

Emily looked up from her camera, curiosity piqued. "You two know each other?"

"We do," Claire said, glancing at Liam. "I met him a while back while working on a piece about Ethan's vineyard and the winemaking community here. I didn't realize at the time that he was such a craftsman."

Liam chuckled. "I didn't realize I'd left much of an impression."

"Oh, you did," Claire teased, turning her attention to Emily. "You must be the photographer Ethan's been raving about. Your work is stunning."

Emily smiled, stepping forward to shake Claire's hand. "Thank you. It's great to meet you."

Over the next hour, the group shared the story of the canoe restoration and the letters Emily had uncovered in the cabin. Claire listened intently, her journal open as she scribbled down notes.

"This story," Claire said, leaning against the workbench, "It's extraordinary. The love between James and Anna, the carvings, the connection to the valley—it deserves to be told. Would you mind if I looked into it further?"

Emily exchanged a glance with Liam, who gave a slight nod. "We'd love that," Emily said. "There are still gaps in the story. If anyone can uncover the rest, that would be great."

Two days later, Claire returned with her findings, excitement radiating from her as she stepped into the boathouse.

"Liam, Emily, you're not going to believe this," she said, holding up an old photograph and a stack of papers.

Ethan, who was visiting, raised an eyebrow. "That's quite the entrance, Claire."

Claire grinned. "Because it's big. I dug through some family records, old archives, and oral histories. It turns out James was my great-uncle."

Emily's jaw dropped. "Wait—what?"

"Yep," Claire confirmed. "My grandmother used to talk about her brother James—the one who disappeared after falling in love with someone the family didn't approve of. She always said he died of heartbreak, but that's not true."

Liam stepped closer, his brow furrowed. "What happened to him?"

Claire laid the photograph on the workbench. It showed a man and woman standing by a lake, a canoe in the background. "They made it. James and Anna escaped across the lake, but they didn't stay in the valley. They kept moving, knowing their families wouldn't stop looking for them. Eventually, they settled further north, in a small community. Quiet, away from the chaos."

Emily's fingers traced the edges of the photo. "So they survived."

"They did," Claire said softly. "They built a life together. My grandmother said James wrote to her once, years later, saying he was happy. He and Anna had a family of their own."

Liam's voice was low, filled with awe. "They found peace. They built the life they wanted."

Emily picked up the photo, studying the couple's expressions. "It's incredible. Their love, their determination—it's all here. And now we get to share it."

Claire nodded, her tone resolute. "This story deserves to be told in full. I've started drafting an article—it's not just about them, but about how love and resilience shaped this valley. It's about honoring what they stood for."

Ethan clapped a hand on Claire's shoulder. "Sounds like you're about to write something unforgettable."

As the group lingered over the photograph, the past and present seemed to converge, the threads of history weaving their stories together. The canoe restoration wasn't just about preserving wood—it was about keeping alive the legacy of love, courage, and connection.

Emily turned to Liam, her voice steady. "This is why we do this. To make sure these stories aren't forgotten."

Liam nodded, his hand brushing over the canoe's smooth surface. "And to remind people of what's worth fighting for."

Chapter 43

Emily and Claire drove up the winding gravel road toward Sammy N'kwala's modest home, nestled in the shade of tall pines. The crisp November air carried the earthy scent of damp leaves and a faint tang of woodsmoke drifting from nearby chimneys.

Sammy had invited them to visit after hearing about their latest discoveries regarding James, Anna, and the canoe restoration.

As they stepped out of the car, Sammy greeted them with his familiar warmth, his lined face breaking into a smile. "Come, sit," he said, gesturing to the wooden chairs on his porch. "The land has stories to share, and so do I."

Emily settled into her chair, her camera resting in her lap, while Claire pulled out her notebook. Sammy's gaze drifted toward the horizon, where the lake shimmered under the afternoon sun.

"You want to know about the Syilx people," Sammy began, his voice steady but layered with emotion. "Our story is tied to this land. It's not just where we lived—it's who we are."

He leaned back, folding his hands over his lap. "The Syilx Okanagan people have been here for thousands of years, long before the settlers arrived. We lived in harmony with the land and the water. The lake was our road, our source of life. We used canoes to fish, to trade, to connect with other communities. Every cedar tree, every stream, every mountain held meaning. It was all connected—like threads in a great woven blanket."

Emily lifted her camera, capturing the thoughtful lines of Sammy's face as he spoke. "How did you live here?" she asked softly.

"Our people were seminomadic," Sammy explained. "We followed the seasons. In the summer, we fished in the lakes and rivers, and in the winter, we sheltered in pithouses called kekuli. These homes were built partially underground, using the earth to keep us warm. They were places of community, of family."

Claire leaned forward, her pen poised over her notebook. "And the canoe? How did it fit into your way of life?"

Sammy smiled faintly, his fingers tracing the arm of his chair. "The canoe was freedom. It was how we moved through the valley, how we gathered food and built relationships. But it was more than that—it was a symbol. Its shape, carved from cedar, reminded us of balance. The lake could be calm or fierce, and the canoe taught us to respect both."

He paused, his gaze distant. "When the settlers came, everything changed. Our people were forced onto reserves. Our language, our traditions—they tried to take them from us. But we are still here. Our stories, our knowledge—they endure."

Emily glanced at Claire, who nodded, urging her to ask the question both of them were wondering. "Sammy," Emily began, "How do you feel about what we're doing? Restoring the canoe, telling James and Anna's story?"

Sammy's expression softened as he looked at her. "You're doing what needs to be done. You're reminding people that this land holds more than dirt and trees. It holds memory. Connection. The canoe Liam restored—it's more than wood and symbols. It's a bridge. A way to bring people back to what matters."

Claire's pen stilled, and she looked up from her notes. "What matters?" she asked, her voice barely above a whisper.

Sammy's eyes shone with quiet wisdom. "That we don't forget who we are. That we honor where we came from and the people who came before us. The Syilx people have always known this, if you care for the land, the land will care for you. That's the lesson we've carried through generations. It's one that everyone needs to remember."

The weight of his words settled over them, heavy with meaning. Emily raised her camera, capturing the moment—not just Sammy's face, but the way the light filtered through the trees behind him, the sense of history that seemed to permeate the air.

Claire reached out, placing a hand on Sammy's arm. "Thank you," she said simply. "For sharing this with us."

Sammy nodded, his voice firm but kind. "It's not just my story. It belongs to the land, to the lake, to the people who still listen. You're part of that now."

As they left Sammy's house later that afternoon, the sun dipping lower in the sky, Emily and Claire driving silently back to the cabin. The words Sammy had spoken lingered, echoing in their minds.

Emily finally broke the silence, her voice quiet but resolute. "I think we need to dig deeper."

Claire nodded, her gaze focused on the horizon. "I agree. For the Syilx, for James and Anna, for everyone who calls this place home."

Chapter 44

The wind outside whispered through the bare branches, carrying with it the first hints of winter. Emily sat across from Claire at the small table in her cabin, a steaming mug of tea between her hands. The painting of James and Anna rested on the table, its edges worn with time.

"So," Emily began, breaking the silence, "What else have you learned about James's family?"

Claire leaned back in her chair, her notebook open in front of her. "It wasn't just about love," she said, her voice measured. "It was about control, legacy, and power. James's family were prominent settlers in the Okanagan back then—landowners, traders, and respected figures in the community. They had everything to gain from maintaining their social status, and everything to lose from a scandal."

Emily frowned, her fingers tracing the edge of her mug. "A scandal, just because he loved Anna?"

Claire nodded. "It's hard to imagine now, but back then, it wasn't just frowned upon—it was considered betrayal. Settlers like James's family didn't see the Syilx people as equals. They believed in preserving their bloodlines, their traditions, their... superiority. A union between James and Anna wasn't just a love story to them—it was a threat to everything they thought they stood for."

Claire's research had painted a vivid picture of the Okanagan in the late 1800s and early 1900s. It was a time of rapid change, as settlers expanded their farms, built railways, and created new towns. The Syilx people, who had lived in harmony with the land for generations, were being forced onto reserves, their way of life disrupted by the influx of settlers and government policies.

"James grew up in privilege," Claire continued. "His family owned land near what's now Carr's Landing. They were well-off, involved in local trade and the early orchard industry. But they were also staunchly traditional, clinging to the idea that their success was tied to their English roots. Marrying a Syilx woman like Anna would have been seen as tarnishing their reputation."

Emily's gaze drifted to the photograph. "And Anna? What about her family?"

"Her family was from one of the Syilx communities near the lake," Claire said, her tone softening. "They lived close to the land, fishing, gathering, and following the seasons. To her people, the lake was sacred—it was life itself. But by the time she met James, her family had already lost much of their land. The settlers had claimed it piece by piece, building fences, railways, and farms. The Syilx were being pushed further and further from the lake, forced to live under conditions they didn't choose."

Emily shook her head. "So neither family approved of them being together."

"No," Claire said, her expression solemn. "For James's family, it was about power and status. For Anna's family, it was about survival. They feared losing what little they had left if she married into a settler's family. And they didn't trust James's intentions—they thought he'd abandon her or use her, like so many settlers had done to Syilx women."

Emily's throat tightened. "It's heartbreaking. They just wanted to be together."

Claire leaned forward, her voice taking on a fervent edge. "But that's what makes their story so powerful, Emily. They risked everything. Anna knew what was at stake— her family, her community, her identity. And James... he gave up his inheritance, his reputation, his entire life for her."

Emily stared at the photograph, imagining the weight they must have carried. "Do you think they knew what they were up against? How hard it would be?"

Claire's expression softened. "I think they did. But love like that doesn't calculate risks. It just moves forward, no matter the cost."

As the evening wore on, Claire shared more details about the Okanagan in those days—the divide between settlers and the Syilx, the tensions over land and resources, and the small but persistent ways in which people like James and Anna defied the odds.

"They weren't the only ones," Claire said quietly. "There were others—settler men and Syilx women who fell in love, despite everything. But most of their stories ended in tragedy. Families were torn apart, children were taken away, and the women were often abandoned, left to navigate a world that didn't see them as worthy."

Emily's heart ached at the thought. "But James and Anna made it. Somehow, they made it."

Claire nodded. "That's why their story matters. It's not just about them—it's about everyone who's ever fought for love in the face of impossible odds. It's about resilience, hope, and the courage to choose your own path."

Later, as Emily sat alone by the fire, her thoughts lingered on the past. The cabin, the lake, the canoe—they all carried the echoes of James and Anna's love, a love that had refused to be defined by the prejudices of its time.

Emily picked up her camera, framing the glow of the fire through the lens. She clicked the shutter, capturing the moment. It wasn't just a photograph—it was a reminder. A promise to honor the stories that deserved to be told.

And as the flames flickered in the hearth, she felt it—the unshakable pull of the Okanagan, a place where love, history, and courage intertwined under the stars.

Chapter 45

The sharp tang of cedar filled the boathouse, mingling with the rhythmic sound of tools against wood. Liam worked with deliberate care, his hands steady as he smoothed the canoe's final touches. Emily stood nearby, her camera poised, capturing the process—the interplay of light and shadow on the grain of the wood, the quiet intensity on Liam's face.

"I still can't get over the fact that your grandfather helped build this canoe," Emily said, lowering her camera. "It's like we're walking in their footsteps."

Liam paused, leaning back on his heels. "It does feel that way. It's strange to think of all the hands that touched this before us—James, Anna, my grandfather. Now us."

Sammy N'kwala arrived just then, his presence grounding as always. He carried a small bundle wrapped in a cloth, which he set gently on the workbench.

"Morning," Sammy said, nodding to them both. "I thought these might help."

Liam unwrapped the bundle carefully, revealing several traditional Syilx tools—chisels, carving knives, and a wooden mallet, all worn with use but lovingly maintained.

"These were my grandfather's," Sammy explained. "He used them to build canoes like this one. They carry his spirit, his knowledge. I think he'd want them to be part of this."

Liam ran his fingers over the tools, reverence in his touch. "Thank you, Sammy. I'll use them with care."

Sammy nodded. "It's not just about the tools, though. It's about the way you use them. The Syilx way of building isn't just physical—it's spiritual. When we shape wood, we listen to it. We respect its strengths and its flaws. The canoe isn't just a vessel, it's a connection between people, the land, and the water."

Emily raised her camera again, capturing the quiet exchange between the two men. "It's incredible," she said softly. "How much meaning is in every step."

Sammy turned to her, his expression thoughtful. "Meaning is in everything, Emily. If you take the time to see it."

The finishing restoration progressed over the next several days, each moment a blend of meticulous work and shared stories. Sammy had guided Liam through traditional techniques—using steam to shape the cedar planks, binding the ribs with natural fibers, and carving intricate patterns into the wood.

"These symbols," Sammy said, tracing a curve on the canoe's hull, "They're not just decorations. They're prayers. For safe passage, for protection, for guidance. Remember, when you carve them, you're asking the land and the water to watch over you."

Liam worked with a focus Emily had rarely seen, his movements careful and precise. She documented each step, the lens of her camera capturing the transformation of the canoe— and of Liam himself.

One evening, as they stood back to admire their progress, Sammy shared another story. "My grandfather used to say that the lake remembers everything. The people who crossed it, the lives it touched. This canoe—it carries those memories. When it's finished, it will carry yours, too."

As the canoe neared completion, the boathouse became a hub of quiet celebration. Ethan stopped by with bottles of wine, marveling at the intricate carvings. Claire arrived with more details about James and Anna's life together, her excitement palpable as she shared her findings.

"They'd be proud of this," Claire said, running a hand along the smooth wood. "You're honoring their story in the best way possible."

Chapter 46

The lake was quiet, its surface a mirror reflecting the starlit sky. Emily and Liam stood at the edge of the boathouse, the restored canoe resting just inside, gleaming in the soft glow of lantern light. The work was done for the day, but neither seemed eager to leave.

"Have you ever seen the stars like this?" Emily asked, her voice barely more than a whisper.

Liam glanced up, his hands tucked into his pockets. "Not like this. It's like they're closer here, brighter somehow."

Emily tilted her head back, her breath visible in the cool November air. "Maybe it's the lake," she mused. "The way it reflects everything. It makes you feel like you're standing in the middle of the universe."

Liam didn't respond right away. Instead, he watched her, the way the starlight caught in her hair, the way her eyes seemed to shine as she gazed at the sky. There was something about her presence—steady yet curious—that had a way of grounding him and pulling him into her orbit all at once.

"Emily," he said quietly, his voice cutting through the stillness.

She turned to him, her brow lifting slightly in question. "What?"

He hesitated, then shook his head, a faint smile playing at his lips. "Nothing. Just... thanks for being here."

Emily smiled softly. "I should be thanking you. This whole experience—it's changed the way I see everything. The valley, the lake, even myself."

Liam stepped closer, his gaze unwavering. "You don't just see things, Emily. You feel them. You bring them to life."

Her cheeks flushed, though she couldn't tell if it was the cold or his words. "You're giving me too much credit. You're the one who—"

"No," Liam interrupted, his voice low but firm. "You don't see it, do you? What you've done here. For me. For the canoe. For all of this."

Emily opened her mouth to respond, but the words caught in her throat. The intensity in his eyes held her captive, the weight of everything unsaid settling between them.

"Liam..." she began, but he took another step closer, closing the distance between them.

"You've made me see things differently, too," he said, his voice softer now, like the lake's gentle lapping against the shore. "I used to think the past was something you could only carry, not change. But you... you've shown me that maybe it's not about changing it. Maybe it's about giving it a voice."

Emily's breath hitched, her heart pounding against her ribs. "I think we've done that for each other."

They stood in silence for a moment, the stars above them and the lake stretching out like an eternity at their feet. Then, slowly, Liam reached out, his fingers brushing against hers. It was a light touch, tentative, but it sent a ripple through her like the lake's reflection breaking across the water.

"Emily," he murmured, his voice barely audible over the soft rustle of the wind. "I don't know what this is, but... I don't want it to end."

She met his gaze, her own eyes shining. "Neither do I."

He stepped closer, his hand sliding into hers with a warmth that chased away the chill of the night. Slowly, he lifted his other hand to her cheek, his touch gentle as though she might vanish if he wasn't careful.

And then, under the vast expanse of the Okanagan sky, he leaned in, his lips meeting hers in a kiss that felt like a promise. It was soft at first, hesitant, but as she leaned into him, her hand resting lightly on his chest, it deepened into something more—a connection that had been quietly building all along.

When they finally broke apart, Emily's breath came in soft, unsteady waves. She looked up at him, her heart full. "It's like the stars," she said softly. "The way they feel closer here. Brighter."

Liam smiled, his thumb brushing lightly against her cheek. "That's how you make me feel."

Emily laughed softly, a sound that was part disbelief, part joy. "You're terrible at this," she teased, though her voice was filled with warmth.

"Probably," Liam admitted, grinning now. "But it's the truth."

They stood there for a while longer, their hands entwined, the world around them fading into the background. For the first time in what felt like forever, Emily wasn't thinking about the past or the future. She was simply here, under the Okanagan stars, with Liam.

Chapter 47

The first rays of dawn broke over the lake, casting a soft pink and gold glow across the water. Emily stirred awake in the cabin, her heart still light from the night before. She could hear the faint lapping of the waves against the shore and the distant calls of birds greeting the morning. Everything felt different—lighter, warmer, as though the air itself had shifted.

A gentle knock at the door pulled her from her thoughts. She smiled, already knowing who it was.

Opening the door, she found Liam standing there, holding two steaming mugs of coffee. His hair was slightly mussed, his flannel shirt unbuttoned over a plain tee, and his smile was soft and unguarded.

"Morning," he said, his voice low and warm.

"Morning," Emily replied, stepping aside to let him in. She accepted one of the mugs, their fingers brushing briefly. "You're up early."

Liam chuckled as he leaned against the counter. "Couldn't sleep. Figured you'd be up too."

She raised an eyebrow. "How'd you know that?"

"You've got that restless energy," he said, his grin teasing but affectionate. "Like you're always ready for the next thing."

Emily laughed softly, taking a sip of the coffee. "Maybe. Or maybe I just don't want to miss the sunrise here. It's like the whole valley wakes up with it."

Liam nodded, his gaze drifting out the window to where the lake shimmered faintly in the morning light. "You're right. There's something about this place. Makes you feel... alive."

Emily watched him for a moment, her heart swelling. She set her mug down and moved closer, her hand brushing against his arm. "Last night," she began, her voice hesitant but sincere, "It felt... right."

Liam turned to her, his eyes searching hers. "It did," he said simply, his hand finding hers.

"I haven't felt that way in a long time, Emily. Like I could just... be."

She smiled, her fingers tightening around his. "Me too. And it scares me a little."

He stepped closer, his other hand brushing a strand of hair from her face. "Me too. But maybe that's a good thing. Maybe it means it's worth it."

Emily exhaled, her tension easing as she leaned into him, resting her forehead against his chest. "I don't know what this is, Liam. But I don't want to lose it."

"You won't," he said firmly, his voice grounding her.

They stood there for a moment, the world outside quiet and still, the warmth between them a quiet promise. Then Liam pulled back, his smile turning mischievous. "Come on, get dressed. There's something I want to show you."

Liam led her down the narrow path that wound from the cabin to the boathouse, the crisp morning air filling their lungs. He stopped at the edge of the dock, motioning for her to wait.

"Close your eyes," he said, a hint of playfulness in his tone.

Emily hesitated, narrowing her eyes at him. "Do I trust you?"

Liam grinned. "I'd hope so."

With a soft laugh, she closed her eyes, letting him guide her a few steps forward. She felt the warmth of the sun on her face, the gentle rocking of the dock beneath her feet, and then his hands on her shoulders, steadying her.

"Okay," he said. "Open them."

Emily opened her eyes and gasped softly. The canoe—their canoe—rested in the water, its polished wood gleaming in the sunlight. The symbols along its hull seemed to glow, as though the lake itself recognized their meaning.

"Liam," she breathed, stepping closer. "It's beautiful."

"Finished it this morning," he said quietly. "I wanted you to see it first, the way it was meant to be seen."

She turned to him, her heart full. "You're incredible, you know that?"

Liam shrugged, his smile shy. "Just trying to keep up with you."

They climbed into the canoe, Liam steadying it as Emily settled onto the bench. He pushed them off the dock, the paddle cutting smoothly through the water as they glided out onto the lake. The world seemed to slow, the only sounds were the rhythmic splash of the paddle and the distant cries of birds.

Emily looked around, taking in the reflection of the mountains and the sky on the still water. "It feels like we're the only two people in the world," she said softly.

"Maybe we are," Liam replied, his voice low. "Out here, it's just us."

Emily turned to him, her gaze steady. "This is magical?"

Liam paused, letting the paddle rest across his knees. "I used to always be planning, always worrying about what was coming. But now... now I just want to be here. With you."

Her breath caught at his words, the sincerity in his voice anchoring her. She reached out, her hand brushing against his. "I know that's what I want too."

Chapter 48

The cabin glowed warmly against the backdrop of the darkening sky, the soft light from the windows spilling onto the gravel path. Inside, the scent of roasting vegetables and freshly baked bread filled the air. Emily moved around the small kitchen, setting plates and glasses on the wooden table, her cheeks pink from the warmth of the oven—and, perhaps, from the stolen glances Liam had been giving her all evening.

"Something smells amazing," Claire said as she stepped inside with Ethan, a bottle of wine in hand. Her gaze swept over the cozy space, landing briefly on the way Liam stood at the counter, sleeves rolled up, helping Emily prepare the meal. She smiled knowingly.

Ethan followed, grinning as he set the wine on the counter. "Look at you two, all domestic," he teased, earning a quick glare from Liam.

"Don't start," Liam warned, though his tone was light.

Claire chuckled as she hung her coat by the door. "We wouldn't dream of it. But I will say—it's nice to see you looking... relaxed, Liam."

Emily glanced over her shoulder, catching Claire's raised eyebrow and subtle smirk. She busied herself with arranging the salad, hiding the slight smile tugging at her lips.

Dinner was lively, the conversation weaving through topics of the vineyard, the gallery exhibit, and the restoration of the canoe. But it wasn't lost on Claire how often Liam and Emily's gazes lingered on one another, or the small, almost unconscious touches they exchanged.

"You've changed," Claire said to Liam, her tone both curious and teasing. "You seem... different. Happier."

Liam glanced at Emily, a soft smile playing at his lips before he shrugged. "Maybe I am."

Ethan raised his glass with a grin. "It's about time."

Emily, caught off guard, flushed and quickly took a sip of her wine.

As the evening wore on, Claire leaned back in her chair, her gaze thoughtful as she studied Liam. "You know, I've never asked—where do you live? It feels like you're always at the boathouse."

Emily perked up, clearly curious about the answer. "That's a good point. I've never seen you leave."

Ethan leaned forward, his grin widening. "Oh, you're going to love this."

Liam shot Ethan a warning look, but his lips twitched with amusement. "There's a loft above the boathouse," he admitted, his tone casual. "That's where I live."

Claire blinked, then laughed softly. "You're kidding."

"Nope," Ethan said, clearly enjoying himself. "It's got everything—bed, stove, the whole works. He's basically married to that boathouse."

Emily looked at Liam, her eyebrows raised. "You live above the boathouse? All this time, and you never mentioned it?"

Liam shrugged, looking slightly sheepish. "It's nothing fancy, but it works. Keeps me close to the projects I'm working on."

Ethan chuckled. "And away from distractions."

Claire tilted her head, a mischievous smile forming. "Seems like distractions are finding their way to you, regardless."

Emily narrowed her eyes at Claire, though she couldn't hide her own grin. "I think it's charming," she said, turning to Liam. "Very... you."

Liam's gaze softened, his smile small but genuine. "Thanks."

As the conversation drifted back to lighter topics, Emily couldn't help but imagine the loft above the boathouse—a space filled with Liam's practical craftsmanship, quiet focus, and perhaps a hint of the warmth she'd come to know in him. It seemed to suit him perfectly.

Later, as the fire crackled in the hearth and the night deepened, Claire leaned toward Emily, her voice low but teasing. "So, do you plan on visiting this infamous loft?"

Emily blushed, her laugh soft but genuine. "Maybe. If I'm invited."

Claire winked, her expression knowing. "Oh, I don't think that'll be a problem."

Across the room, Ethan nudged Liam with a playful grin. "Looks like you've got company for that loft of yours."

Liam gave a low laugh, shaking his head, but his gaze found Emily's, and the unspoken connection between them was undeniable.

The evening ended with hugs and promises to meet again soon. As Ethan and Claire drove away, Emily stood at the cabin door, watching the taillights disappear into the night. Liam joined her, his hand resting lightly on her back.

"They're good people," Emily said softly.

"They are," Liam agreed, his voice warm. "But I'm glad they've gone."

Emily looked up at him, her smile teasing. "Why's that?"

Liam leaned closer, his voice low. "Because now it's just us."

Chapter 49

The cabin was quiet, the fire crackling softly in the hearth, its warm glow casting flickering shadows across the walls. Emily leaned against the counter, her heart racing as Liam stood just a few feet away, his tall frame silhouetted against the firelight. He had stayed late, the hours slipping by as they shared stories and laughter, their connection deepening with every passing moment.

But now, the air between them was charged, thick with unspoken words and possibilities.

"You don't have to go," Emily said softly, her voice barely above a whisper.

Liam turned to her, his gaze steady and intense. For a moment, he didn't say anything, and Emily felt the weight of his eyes on her, as though he was seeing her completely—every flaw, every vulnerability, every spark of desire.

"Are you sure?" he asked, his voice low and rough.

Emily swallowed, her pulse quickening. "Yes."

He crossed the room in a few strides, his presence filling the space around her. Gently, he reached out, his fingers brushing a strand of hair from her face. "You have no idea how long I've wanted this," he murmured.

Her breath hitched as she looked up at him, her voice trembling with honesty. "I think I do."

And then he kissed her.

It wasn't tentative or hesitant—it was a kiss that spoke of all the moments they had held back, all the feelings they had tried to suppress. His hands cupped her face, tilting her head as his lips moved against hers, and Emily felt herself melting into him, her hands gripping the front of his shirt as though afraid to let go.

Liam broke the kiss just long enough to rest his forehead against hers, his breath warm against her skin. "Tell me if this is too fast," he said, his voice ragged.

Emily shook her head, her fingers curling into his shirt. "No. It's exactly right."

With that, he kissed her again, deeper this time, his hands sliding down to her waist and pulling her closer. The world outside the cabin faded into nothingness—the lake, the stars, the chill of the November night. All that mattered was the heat building between them, the way their bodies seemed to fit together as though they had been waiting for this moment all along.

Emily's hands moved of their own accord, slipping under the fabric of his shirt to feel the warmth of his skin, the hard lines of muscle beneath her fingertips. Liam groaned softly against her mouth, his own hands exploring the curve of her back, the softness of her waist.

"Emily," he murmured, her name a prayer on his lips. "You're... incredible."

She laughed softly, the sound breathless and full of wonder. "You're not so bad yourself."

Liam's lips curved into a smile before he kissed her again, his hands lifting her effortlessly onto the counter. Emily gasped at the sudden shift, her legs instinctively wrapping around his waist as he stepped between her knees. His hands roamed over her, his touch both gentle and possessive, and Emily felt a heat rising in her that had nothing to do with the fire in the hearth.

Time seemed to blur as they lost themselves in each other, every kiss, every touch igniting something deeper. Liam's shirt hit the floor, followed by hers, the cool air brushing against her skin before his hands warmed her again. Emily pulled him closer, her fingers tangling in his hair as his lips trailed along her jaw, down her neck, leaving a trail of fire in their wake.

"Stay," she whispered, her voice trembling with need.

Liam paused, his gaze meeting hers. There was no hesitation in his eyes, only a deep, unshakable certainty. "Always."

He lifted her effortlessly, carrying her toward the bed, the cabin filled with the soft rustle of movement and the sound of their breathing, quick and shallow. The world outside ceased to exist as they surrendered to each other completely, their connection was no longer just emotional but physical, and their bodies moved in perfect harmony.

Later, as they lay tangled together under the blankets, the firelight casting a warm glow over their bare skin, Emily traced lazy circles on Liam's chest, her head resting against his shoulder.

"Do you think this changes everything?" she asked softly.

Liam kissed the top of her head, his voice a low rumble. "I think it changes nothing and everything at the same time."

Emily smiled, her heart full. "That's a very Liam answer."

He chuckled, the sound vibrating through her. "What I mean is, it doesn't change how I feel about you. But it does make me want more. More of this. More of us."

Emily tilted her head to look up at him, her smile soft. "I know I want that too."

As the fire crackled softly and the stars outside shone brightly, they fell into a peaceful silence, their breaths syncing, their hearts beating as one. For the first time in a long time, Emily felt truly at home—not just in the cabin or the valley, but in Liam's arms.

And under the Okanagan stars, she knew they had found something worth holding onto.

Chapter 50

The first signs of spring had transformed the Okanagan Valley. Vibrant greens began to creep across the hillsides, replacing the muted tones of winter. Wildflowers peeked from the edges of trails, and the crisp air carried the sweet, faint scent of blooming cherry blossoms.

Emily stood at the edge of the lake, her boots crunching softly against the gravel as she adjusted her camera. The lake sparkled under the bright morning sun, and across its glassy surface, the mountains seemed more alive, their slopes dotted with fresh growth. It was a new season, and with it came new energy—a promise of change and renewal.

Behind her, Liam's voice broke through the quiet. "You've been out here since sunrise."

She turned, smiling at the sight of him walking toward her. His hair was slightly tousled from the breeze, his flannel shirt rolled to his elbows, revealing the strength in his forearms. He carried two mugs of coffee, steam curling into the cool morning air.

"You say that like it's a bad thing," she replied, accepting the coffee gratefully.

"It's not," Liam said with a grin, his eyes softening as he looked at her. "Just wondering if you've even noticed it's spring."

Emily laughed, taking a sip of her coffee. "How could I not? It's everywhere. The whole valley feels like it's waking up."

Liam nodded, his gaze drifting out to the water. "It's my favorite time of year. Everything feels... possible."

She tilted her head, studying him. "Even us?"

He glanced at her, his smile deepening. "Especially us."

The weeks since winter had passed quietly, their days blending into a rhythm of shared work and stolen moments. Emily had spent her time capturing the first signs of spring, her camera lens seeking the subtle shifts in the landscape. Liam had thrown himself into the boatbuilding workshops he'd started, the boathouse now filled with the hum of tools and the chatter of eager students.

The Lady of the Lake restoration had become a centerpiece of their shared efforts, with Sammy stopping by regularly to check on its progress. Together, they had decided to display it at an upcoming community event—a celebration of the valley's heritage and its enduring spirit.

As they walked back toward the cabin, Emily glanced at Liam, her heart swelling at the sight of him so at ease. "How's the boathouse holding up with all the students?"

Liam smirked. "Crowded. I've got wood shavings in places I didn't know they could get. But it's worth it. Watching people learn, seeing their faces light up when they figure something out—it's a good feeling."

Emily smiled, nudging him lightly. "You're a natural teacher."

He glanced at her, his expression serious. "I've been learning from you, you know."

She raised an eyebrow. "Me?"

"Yeah," he said, his voice warm. "You've got this way of seeing things—finding the beauty in places most people overlook. It's made me want to look closer, to pay more attention."

Emily's cheeks flushed, but she held his gaze. "And you've taught me to slow down. To appreciate the process, not just the result."

They reached the cabin, its porch now adorned with pots of early spring flowers that Emily had picked up from a nearby nursery. She set her coffee down and turned to Liam, her hands sliding into his.

"I think we make a good team," she said softly.

Liam smiled, his thumbs brushing over her knuckles. "We do. And it feels like we're just getting started."

That evening, as the sun dipped behind the mountains and the valley was bathed in soft twilight, Emily and Liam sat on the porch, the air filled with the sound of crickets and the occasional splash of water from the lake. A gentle breeze rustled the budding leaves, carrying with it the scent of earth and renewal.

"It's amazing how fast time goes," Emily mused, her head resting on Liam's shoulder.

He wrapped an arm around her, pulling her closer. "Yeah, but this—this feels like it's moving at just the right pace."

She smiled, her gaze drifting to the lake. "Spring feels different this year. Like it's not just about the seasons changing, it's about us, too."

Liam pressed a kiss to the top of her head. "Because it is. This place, this time—it's all ours now."

As the stars began to emerge, casting their light over the valley, Emily felt a quiet contentment settle over her. The past was still a part of her, but it no longer defined her. And the future, though uncertain, felt like something worth embracing.

Under the Okanagan sun, in the bloom of spring, she realized that they had found something rare—a love that grew as naturally as the seasons themselves.

Chapter 51

The late spring sun shone brightly over the Okanagan, the gentle breeze carrying the scent of fresh blossoms and the soft rustle of water lapping against the shore. The boathouse stood adorned with garlands of greenery and wildflowers, a rustic yet elegant backdrop for the ceremony that was about to take place. Friends and family gathered along the lakeshore, their laughter and quiet chatter filling the air.

Emily stood inside the boathouse, her heart fluttering as Claire adjusted the delicate lace of her gown. The dress was simple yet breathtaking, its flowing fabric brushing the floor as Emily shifted her weight nervously.

"You're beautiful," Claire said, her voice filled with warmth. "Liam's not going to know what hit him."

Emily laughed softly, the sound shaky with emotion. "I feel like I might float away."

"Good thing you've got Liam to anchor you," Claire teased, giving her a reassuring smile. "You ready?"

Emily took a deep breath and nodded. "As ready as I'll ever be."

Outside, Liam stood at the makeshift altar in front of the boathouse, the Lady of the Lake resting quietly in the water nearby, its polished wood gleaming in the sunlight. He wore a crisp white shirt with the sleeves rolled up and a simple boutonniere pinned to his chest. Ethan stood beside him, grinning like he was the one getting married.

"You nervous?" Ethan asked under his breath.

Liam glanced at him, his expression steady. "Not even a little."

Ethan chuckled. "Of course not. You're about to marry the woman who makes you look like a better version of yourself."

Liam smirked. "Isn't that what you're supposed to do?"

Before Ethan could reply, the soft strains of a violin began to play, and the guests turned toward the boathouse. Emily stepped out, her arm linked with Sammy's, who had offered to walk her down the aisle. The elder wore a traditional Syilx vest, his face glowing with quiet pride.

As Emily's eyes met Liam's, the rest of the world seemed to fade away. He watched her with an intensity that made her heart skip a beat, his love for her written in every line of his face.

When she reached him, Sammy placed her hand in Liam's and stepped back with a small nod, his approval unspoken but deeply felt.

The ceremony was simple but heartfelt. Henry read a poem about the lake, his voice steady despite the emotion that flickered in his eyes. Claire and Ethan exchanged playful glances as they handed the rings to Liam and Emily. When Liam spoke his vows, his voice steady but filled with emotion, there wasn't a dry eye in the crowd.

"Emily," he said, his hands warm around hers, "You've shown me what it means to see the world through fresh eyes. To find beauty in the simple things. You're my compass, my anchor, and my home. I promise to love you, to honor this life we're building, and to never stop seeing you the way I do right now."

Emily's voice trembled as she spoke her vows. "Liam, you've given me a reason to believe again. You've taught me to slow down, to cherish the journey as much as the destination. I promise to stand by your side, to celebrate your dreams as our own, and to love you with all that I am."

When they kissed, the cheers and applause echoed across the lake, blending with the calls of birds and the soft breeze that carried the scent of wildflowers.

As the sun dipped lower in the sky, painting the lake in shades of gold and amber, Liam led Emily to the dock where the Lady of the Lake waited. The guests waved and cheered as they stepped aboard, the boat rocking gently beneath them.

Liam untied the ropes and pushed them off the dock, the sail catching the evening breeze as they glided across the water. Emily leaned against him, her fingers intertwined with his, her heart full.

"This is perfect," she said softly. "I don't think I've ever been this happy."

Liam smiled, his arm wrapping around her shoulders. "Me neither."

They drifted in comfortable silence for a while, the shoreline growing smaller as the lake stretched endlessly around them. Then, suddenly, Emily looked up at him, a thought breaking through her reverie.

"Liam," she said, her brow furrowing slightly. "Where are we going to live?"

He glanced at her, a teasing glint in his eye. "At the cabin."

Emily blinked. "The cabin?"

He nodded, his grin widening. "I've owned it for years."

Her jaw dropped slightly. "You've owned the cabin this whole time? And you didn't think to tell me?"

Liam laughed, pulling her closer. "I figured it'd come up eventually. Besides, I like surprises."

Emily stared at him for a moment before bursting into laughter, the sound carrying over the water. "Hey wait, its you I have been paying rent to all this time!"

"And you love me anyway," Liam said, his tone warm and teasing.

She leaned up, pressing a kiss to his lips. "I do. More than anything."

As the Lady of the Lake sailed under the Okanagan setting sun, Emily rested her head against Liam's chest, the future stretched out before them like the calm, endless water. They had found their place—together. And it felt like the beginning of their own chapter in the timeless story of the Okanagan.

Poems

Beautiful B.C.

The West wind is blowing
And calling to me,
Come back to the mountains,
Come back to the sea,
Green valleys in blossom
With blue skies above,
I'll always come home
To this land that I love.

There is gold in the sunset
Where wild geese still fly,
Where proud Douglas fir trees
Are ever reaching to the sky,
And wild rushing rivers
Run down to the sea.
Dear land of the dogwood,
Our Beautiful B.C.

The wild flowers are blooming,
So fragrant and fair,
From meadow and hillside
They perfume the air,
And small creeks are rippling,
Their waters so cool,

Where cattle are grazing
By deep shady pools.

Your smoky blue mountains
With white crowning snow,
Your emerald green islands
Where gentle ocean breezes blow,
Your dark northern forests
I'm longing to see.
Dear land of the dogwood,
Our Beautiful B.C.

Frank Brummet *(my father-in-law)*

Lake Okanagan

Oh! Unpredictable beautiful lake.
Smooth as a millpond one moment,
Then suddenly angry and turbulent.
Driving boaters and fishermen into shore.

Beloved lake, you have brought sadness
Yet so much happiness too.
To swim, to row, feathering my oars with you.
Lovely enjoyable trips on the sternwheeler.
Boys on the wharf diving for coins in your
clear waters.
Memories of the thirties, with the ferry
icebound.
Crossing the lake on foot, we passengers of
the greyhound.
Following our driver, pulling a sleigh with
luggage,
My small daughter a passenger too.

Our lake, heaving, groaning, with the whistling
windy weather,
Yet, giving us safe passage across.
Like our surrounding hills, our lovely lake will
live on forever.

Jessie B. Fletcher *(my paternal grandmother)*

Acknowledgments

*W*riting *Under the Okanagan Sun* has been a journey of creativity, reflection, and deep appreciation for the people and places that made this story possible.

First and foremost, I want to express my heartfelt gratitude to my family for their unwavering love, patience, and belief in me. Growing up in the Okanagan, I was surrounded by its quiet beauty, and your support gave me the freedom to revisit those cherished landscapes and explore the themes of love, legacy, and healing that shape this novel.

A special thank you to the **Okanagan Valley**—its breathtaking landscapes, sparkling lake views, rugged cedar groves, and vibrant communities provided both the backdrop and heartbeat of this story. The region's rich history and timeless charm inspired every word, every scene, and every thread of connection woven into this tale.

To the Syilx Okanagan heritage and stories, I offer my deepest respect and gratitude. Your enduring connection to the land, water, and traditions influenced the soul of this novel and reminded me of the importance of honoring the past while moving forward with care and intention.

To my mentors, colleagues, and fellow writers—thank you for your encouragement, insight, and thoughtful feedback. Your guidance helped me shape this story with authenticity and depth.

To my readers, thank you for stepping into the world of *Under the Okanagan Sun.* It is my hope that this story resonates with your hearts, inspires reflection, and reminds you of the beauty found in resilience, connection, and the courage to follow your dreams.

Finally, I extend my gratitude to the creative spirit that continues to guide my writing and to the timeless stories of the Okanagan—ones that whisper through its lakes, its mountains, and its people. Writing *Under the Okanagan Sun* has been a celebration of history, hope, and the ties that bind us to the land and to one another.

With deepest thanks,

Dr. Constance Santego

The Author

Dr. Constance Santego

Dr. Constance Santego is a celebrated author, educator, and holistic healer whose work seamlessly blends storytelling with themes of love, healing, and personal growth. With a doctorate in Natural Medicine and decades of experience in the healing arts, Constance brings a unique depth to her writing, guiding readers on journeys of both heart and soul.

Growing up in the Okanagan Valley, surrounded by its natural beauty and rich history, Constance developed a deep-rooted connection to the land she calls home. Her father's grandparents settled in Vernon in

1912, and her mother's family arrived in Kelowna in 1944, establishing generations of ties to the region. This heritage inspires Constance's novels, where the stunning landscapes, vibrant communities, and untold stories of the Okanagan shine through every page.

In her latest work, *Under the Okanagan Sun,* Constance transports readers to Kelowna's rolling vineyards, serene lake shores, and hidden cedar groves. Through themes of legacy, connection, and transformation, she invites readers to rediscover the beauty of resilience and the enduring power of love against the backdrop of the valley's timeless charm.

When she's not writing, Constance enjoys life with her husband in Kelowna, where she finds inspiration in the quiet moments by the lake, exploring local history, and fostering personal growth in those around her. Whether through her stories, teachings, or explorations, she remains dedicated to her mission: to craft narratives that heal, uplift, and connect us all.